C.H.A.R.O.N.

A NIGHT VIGIL NOVEL: BOOK TWO

GAIL Z. MARTIN

SOL

CONTENTS

C.H.A.R.O.N.

A NIGHT VIGIL NOVEL: BOOK TWO

By Gail Z. Martin

eBook ISBN: 978-1-64795-033-0
Print ISBN: 978-1-64795-034-7

SOL Publishing is an imprint of DreamSpinner Communications, LLC

For my readers. Because you read, I write.

CHAPTER ONE

UNSEEN HANDS LIFTED Brent Lawson and threw him across the room to land hard against a rusted piece of equipment.

"Chant faster!" he yelled, staggering to his feet.

Travis Dominick never paused, reciting the banishment ritual from memory. He held up a crucifix in his right hand and flipped off his ghost hunting partner with his left.

The temperature in the abandoned blast furnace hovered around freezing, cold enough that Travis could see his breath as he spoke the litany. Their vengeful ghost had grown strong over the years, and while Travis sympathized with the specter's grievance, the attacks had to stop.

"Release the anger that binds you to this world," Travis intoned, trying not to be distracted as he glimpsed Brent flying across the room once more. "Accept your death, let go of vengeance, and go into the light."

"Just tell him to get the fuck out!" Brent shouted, shaking himself off as he climbed to his feet again. He racked his shotgun and sent a blast of rock salt into the air in the direction his ghostly assailant had last been visible.

Cold wind swept through the steel mill, and the strong push of spectral hands came from a different angle, sending Brent stumbling.

"Go to hell, you fucker!" Brent shot again, and this time an angry screech echoed through the abandoned mill.

"Oliver Grant, I abjure your spirit and bind your soul. Let go of this mortal world and move on. In the name of the Holy Trinity and the Apostles, let it be so!" Travis finished the banishment, but another blast from Brent's shotgun told him that Oliver's ghost wasn't going to cooperate.

The salt circle around him bought Travis time, keeping Oliver from attacking as he tried to send the spirit on its way. Brent played defense, trying to distract the ghost and draw its fire. Unfortunately, Oliver clung to the place of his death with single-minded tenacity.

Travis and Brent researched the ghost before heading for the old mill. Oliver had been a foreman and came to his shift unsteady on his feet one night in 1967. Whether Oliver was ill or drunk seemed a matter for debate, but he had tumbled into a cauldron of molten steel, which cremated him alive.

The sullied steel should have been discarded. It hadn't been and instead was molded into I-beams used in the expansion of that same mill. Oliver's ghost never left. The haunting eased when the mill closed, but the recent demolition of some buildings on the lot seemed to have woken the spirit.

What the hell were they thinking using that steel? I can't blame Oliver for staying, but the people he's hurting had nothing to do with his fall. Several recent deaths among construction workers on the site seemed directly linked to Oliver, and Travis suspected the ghost's involvement in other equipment malfunctions and accidents.

Oliver's ghost materialized in front of Travis, glowering with hatred. He matched the few photos Travis had found—a scowling, stocky man in his middle years with a shock of unruly white hair and the face of a boxer. From what Travis and Brent pieced together, Oliver had been an angry, miserable person and an overly demanding boss long before his accident.

So much so that Travis wondered if Oliver had been pushed. *Not that he needed help becoming a vengeful spirit.*

The ghost's image broke up like static on a bad TV channel. Travis could not mistake the malice in the spirit's smirk. The image flickered and appeared in front of Brent, rushed him, and knocked the gun out of his grasp. Oliver's hands closed around Brent's throat, and Travis did not doubt that the ghost intended to kill.

Fuck you. Travis launched into the Rite of Exorcism, something he had hoped to avoid. While the banishment ritual wasn't gentle with wayward spirits, the exorcism—designed to send demons back to Hell—was brutal.

Oliver deserved a bum's rush to the afterlife, and Travis intended to deliver it.

"*Exorcizamos te, omnis immundus spiritus...*" Travis began, rattling off the familiar Latin.

Oliver's spirit flickered as Travis continued the rite.

Brent scrabbled to grab a piece of steel behind him and swung it through the ghost's torso. It broke the spirit's hold on his throat, letting him twist away.

Oliver screeched, and his image blurred. But as Travis read the rest of the exorcism, Oliver struggled to re-form. It looked to Travis as if something snatched away parts of the ghost, unraveling him like peeling an apple.

"What have you done to me?" Oliver shrieked. His voice sounded thinner, more distant. The image faded as the tendrils stripped by the exorcism unraveled his soul.

"Not nearly what you deserve." Brent's voice was still raspy from being choked.

"*Ut inimicos sanctae Ecclesiae humiliare digneris, te rogamus, audi nos!*

"No! You can't! I'm not finished—" Oliver's shouts grew fainter as his spirit faded, and the last of the ghost finally vanished.

Travis breathed a sigh of relief, and the psychic exertion of the ritual left him drained and hollowed. He searched the shop floor for his partner.

"Brent?"

Brent staggered from the shadows into the sullied light spilling from the filthy, broken windows. "Still alive. D'ya think that exorcism would work if you recorded it and played it double-speed?"

Travis looked at his friend and shook his head with fond concern. "Not a bad idea. We can try it. Of course, if it doesn't work, we'll both die. But hey—worth a shot?"

Brent rolled his eyes. "Next time, you fight off the ghost, and I'll read the fancy Latin."

"You're forgetting the whole ex-priest thing," Travis pointed out. "Bit of an advantage on the exorcism."

"Show off," Brent muttered, but his attitude reassured Travis that his hunting partner wasn't too badly hurt.

"You okay?"

Brent nodded, then winced. "I've had worse. But the bruises are gonna be spectacular."

"Let's go back to St. Dismas. Matthew can patch you up."

Brent's resigned sigh told Travis all he needed to know about his friend's condition. "All right. Do you think there's anything left from dinner? I'm starving."

Travis chuckled. "If not, there's always peanut butter and jelly and hot tea to wash it down with. Can you walk?"

Brent took a few limping steps. "I'm not going to be entering any dance contests, but I can make it to the car."

"Matthew will want to keep an eye on you for a concussion. It's movie night for the residents. How about we eat, watch a good flick, and you can crash on my couch," Travis suggested.

"Sounds like a plan."

Travis noticed how Brent winced when he bent to get into Travis's old Crown Victoria. He wondered if Brent was hurt more than he let on. *Typical ex-soldier.*

"Do you think Oliver will stay gone?" Brent asked.

"The exorcism on top of the banishment should make it permanent," Travis replied. "But just to be sure, I'll get some friends to pull a few strings, report that the new section that used the contaminated steel is a biohazard. That means it will be dismantled and sealed in concrete. We'll add supernatural protections. That should do it."

"You hope."

Travis shrugged. "We don't get a lot of certainty in this business. I'll take what I can get." He glanced at the clock. "We'll have missed dinner at St. Dismas. How about we stop at Folsom Diner? We can grab a bite to eat and see one of my contacts."

"You need to see one of your Night Vigil people?"

"Yeah. Darius called and said he had a warning for me. Since his 'tips' have never been wrong, I figured I'd better go see what he has to say."

The "Night Vigil" was Travis's name for the misfit collection of people with untrained paranormal skills he sought out and tried to save. Having a supernatural skill that went unrecognized, reviled, and denied took a toll. Most of the people Travis had cobbled into a loosely knit found family had damaged themselves and others and now desperately needed a way to atone.

Folsom Diner sat in the Strip District, an area along the Allegheny River where ships and trucks delivered produce, fresh fish, and other bulk items to the wholesalers that provisioned restaurants and caterers. Since the shipments came in at all hours, the diner was open round the clock to serve hungry truckers and sailors. The food was good, plentiful, and affordable.

A handful of tired men in flannel shirts filled seats in the diner long after the dinner rush had ended. The smell of coffee, bacon, and French fries hung in the air. The glass cooler case full of cakes and pies greeted them at the register and offered the possibility of sugar resurrection, especially paired with a bottomless cup of java.

"Coffee," Travis ordered for both of them when the server came to their booth. "Just leave the pot. Bring dessert first. I want the coconut cake."

"I'll take the lemon meringue pie," Brent said, holding his cup in both hands like the elixir of life. "And then the burger Blue Plate."

"Same," Travis added, figuring simple was best. "And is Darius working tonight?"

The server—her name tag read "Trish"—tucked her notepad into her apron. "Yeah. He's bussing tables. Should be going on break any time now."

"Can you tell him that Travis dropped in, please?" He managed a smile. "I'd sure appreciate it."

Trish nodded like she was too damn tired to care. "Sure. If I see him, I'll tell him."

"Dunno if I'd bet money on that," Brent said after Trish was out of earshot.

"I texted Darius. Trish was backup," Travis replied with a shrug.

The adrenaline drop after a near-death experience on a hunt wasn't a surprise after all these years. Travis had been hunting monsters and dealing with malicious supernatural creatures since his mid-twenties when he took his vows for the priesthood and swore his oath to the Sinistram, a shadowy secret Vatican organization that dealt with all things paranormal.

He'd left the Church and cut ties with the Sinistram nearly a decade later, burned out and disillusioned, angry over the betrayals of trust he'd witnessed and experienced. He walked away from the cassock and collar but not the work of fighting evil. So now he ran St. Dismas, a halfway house in a tough neighborhood named for the penitent thief at the Crucifixion, and hunted monsters on the side.

"Father Travis."

Travis looked up to see Darius standing beside the table and slid over to make room for him on the bench. "Just Travis. Hi, Darius. This is Brent, my hunting partner," he added with a nod toward his companion. "You said you had something to tell me?"

Darius looked to be in his early twenties, still struggling with acne and confidence. A hairnet covered his locs. He wore a black polo shirt, jeans, and a dishwasher's apron, and his hands looked chapped from too much time in water.

"Yeah. You said to tell you—"

"You did the right thing," Travis assured him. "What's up?"

Darius looked around nervously, perhaps making sure no one was close enough to overhear. "Don't cross the bridge."

Travis frowned. "What bridge?"

Darius shook his head. "I don't know. The images I see—they don't always make sense. Like catching a minute out of a TV show you've never seen before. There was a highway bridge with woods and a river. Except that the far side of the bridge went into fire and darkness—like Hell."

Shit. Does he know how many bridges there are in the whole fucking state of Pennsylvania?

"Were there other details? An unusual building or a big sign—something?" Travis didn't doubt Darius's precognition, but without more to go on, the tip was too broad to be useful.

Darius squeezed his eyes shut, and Travis guessed the young man was trying to concentrate on his memory of the vision. "South," he said finally. "Painted on a big wall on a building you can see from the bridge." He sighed. "Sorry. It's not much. But you said—"

"It's fine." Travis saw how skittish Darius was and guessed he feared they would think he had wasted their time. "Visions usually don't make sense until all the pieces come together. We'll know to keep an eye out, and it might save our lives. This is exactly what I meant when I told you to call me when you had a tip, no matter what."

Darius nodded, and his Adam's apple bobbed. "Okay. Good. I just want to help."

Buried in the earnestness, Travis recognized guilt and the desperate need for absolution. He knew Darius's story, how he had ignored premonitions that ended up costing lives because his ability bewildered and frightened him. The Church had terrified him, made him fear hellfire, and because of that, people died. *Just one more reason I left that all behind.*

For years, the Sinistram held Travis's ability as a medium over his head, threatening excommunication or worse. When he realized he no longer cared, he walked away free.

"Your ability is a good thing," Travis told Darius. "Don't ever let anyone tell you otherwise."

Darius nodded, but Travis saw the doubt in his eyes and hoped that someday it would fade.

"If you *see* anything else, please call," Travis urged. Darius ducked his head and nodded, then vanished into the kitchen.

"If we're going to avoid bridges, we aren't going far in Pennsylvania," Brent said when Darius was gone.

"We both know how visions work," Travis replied. Brent's ghostly twin brother, Danny, used to pass along warnings from the other side, and Travis's Night Vigil friends shared information that had saved their lives many times.

"They're a real bitch. Too much information to let someone sleep at night, not enough to always help avoid what they saw," Brent agreed. "At least your ghosts talk."

Travis snorted. "Sometimes. Or they talk in riddles. It's not like they just lay the whole issue out there. Nothing paranormal is simple."

Trish brought their dessert and assured them the burgers wouldn't be far behind. Brent moved as if every muscle hurt, and a bruise on the left side of his face would probably be spectacular come morning.

Travis knew Brent wouldn't admit how much he was hurting, but he could see the way the other man winced when he moved and bit back a groan as sore muscles protested.

When they finished eating, Travis paid the check and hustled

Brent to the car. "Let's have Matthew take a look and make sure it's not worse than sore muscles. He can give you something for the discomfort."

"I'm okay."

"*Sure* you are."

They drove to St. Dismas, and Travis felt glad that Brent had agreed to stay over. He knew his partner was hurt worse than he let on and was grateful that Brent relented enough to allow St. Dismas's medic check for serious injuries.

Matthew was ex-Army, like Brent. Travis resigned himself to the fact that their shared experience led to an unspoken understanding he would never fully fathom. *As long as Matthew gets Brent to take care of himself, I don't mind being odd man out.*

Travis still felt surprised when he thought about the past year; how he had gone from working alone to finding a partner, one with whom he was exceptionally in sync despite their disparate backgrounds. They had hated each other in their first encounter, then grudgingly moved to mutual respect and discovered they made a good team. Travis now counted Brent as one of his closest friends, a "brother by another mother" as it were.

"How do you feel? *Really,*" Travis asked as he pulled into his parking space at St. Dismas, one of the few perks of management he permitted himself.

"Like I was hit by a bus and dragged for a few miles over cobblestones," Brent growled.

"Okay. Don't bite. I texted Matthew while we were at the restaurant. He's expecting us. He'll get you patched up and give you something for the pain."

Brent's grunt signaled agreement, even though he shook off Travis's helping hand to assist him from the car into the building.

Jon, Travis's second-in-command, waited at the door. "What's the damage? How can I help?"

Travis and Jon were an odd pair. At thirty-three and six-foot-two,

Travis was solid, lean muscle, with chin-length black hair and green eyes that were in sharp contrast to the pale coloring of his Irish heritage. Jon was five-ten and forty-something, built like a fireplug, with close-cropped dark hair, wary eyes, and chestnut skin. Jon had been an Army chaplain before St. Dismas, and his military background still showed itself in his movements and tone.

"Brent got thrown around while I banished the spirit," Travis replied, hovering close in case the other man collapsed. "Matthew better check for a concussion, fractured ribs, and broken bones. Brent's going to need something for the pain."

"I'm okay," Brent protested futilely, although the way he winced from movement and his quick, sharp breathing put the lie to his protests.

"I'll judge that." Matthew Sanchez joined them in the corridor, a wiry man in his early thirties with thick black hair and stubble. "Let's have a look."

Brent followed Matthew to the shelter's small clinic, which could handle minor illnesses and injuries to help their residents—and Travis—avoid trips to the emergency room. Travis waited in the hallway, letting Brent have some privacy.

"Rough night?" Jon pressed a cup of coffee into Travis's hands.

"Could have gone better—but it also might have been a whole lot worse," Travis conceded. Both Jon and Matthew knew about his "extra-curricular" activities hunting monsters. "But we got the job done."

"Do I need to scrounge up food for you?" Jon asked.

Travis shook his head. "We ate. Although if we're making popcorn for movie night, might be good to make a little extra."

"I think we can manage that," Jon replied. "The beds are full tonight, and the guys seemed excited about the movie. Or maybe just the popcorn."

"Both, I'm sure," Travis said. St. Dismas was—as far as most people were aware—a halfway house, soup kitchen, food bank, and shelter, a last-chance outpost for tired souls seeking refuge. Being Travis's base of operations for hunting was a well-kept secret.

Matthew opened the door after a while and motioned for them to come inside. The room smelled like liniment. Brent sat shirtless on the exam table, his chest and back covered with bruises. He looked haggard for only being in his early thirties. Though he had been out of the military for years, his muscular build suggested boot camp rather than gym rat. The cut of his blond hair said "civilian," but the way he sat, poised to spring at the first sign of threat, said "military."

"Nothing broken," Matthew told them after a nod from Brent. "But the pulled muscles are going to hurt like a mofo. I've given him heavy-duty ibuprofen and something for the pain—at least for tonight."

Matthew gave Brent a stern look. "Don't mix the pain meds with alcohol."

Brent frowned. "Not my first rodeo."

"Won't be a problem tonight," Travis assured the medic. Out of respect for their residents who struggled with sobriety, Travis didn't permit any alcohol on site, even in his apartment. He didn't have a personal objection to drinking and would share a few with Brent when they were elsewhere, but he was glad that for tonight he could make sure Brent didn't do any "self-medicating."

Travis tried not to notice how Brent hobbled toward the multi-purpose room, and he slowed his stride to accommodate.

"Quit hovering," Brent crabbed.

"Just being polite."

Brent grumbled, apparently not in agreement. That made Travis smile because if Brent felt well enough to be curmudgeonly, he wasn't on death's doorstep.

Jon already had the big room set up with rows of chairs, a table with chips, popcorn, and pitchers of Lemon Blennd on one side, and a big screen in front. Most of the seats were already full, so Travis and Brent slid into the last row. From the buzz of conversation, Travis knew his pick of movies had been a good fit. *Light on plot, plenty of action and explosions. Perfect for a Friday night.*

The chatter quieted once the movie began. Jon kept the volume reasonable to reduce the risk of loud noises triggering any of the residents with PTSD. While that technically also included him and Brent, Travis knew their triggers lay elsewhere. It made him happy to see their residents enjoying the movie, putting aside their worries for a little while.

Brent shuffled in his seat, clearly trying to get comfortable.

"We can leave if you want to," Travis whispered, realizing that the hard plastic chairs probably weren't helping Brent's sore body.

"I'm all right," Brent muttered. Travis knew the action flick was one of Brent's favorites, which might make him willing to put up with the discomfort.

Halfway through, Travis nudged Brent when he snored loudly. Brent flailed and nearly tumbled from his chair. Travis muffled a snicker.

"Come on, you're falling asleep."

"Am not."

"You snore louder than the explosions," Travis whispered. "You'll be more comfortable on the couch. This is a tough crowd—they might throw popcorn."

"Okay, okay." Brent sounded like a grumpy child.

They slipped out of the room, and Brent followed Travis to his quarters. St. Dismas took over a hard-luck hotel, renovating and repurposing the spaces. Travis and Jon both had small apartments in the building so they could serve as live-in coordinators. Matthew had a place nearby, while Brent's house was on the South Side.

"Home, sweet home," Travis announced as he turned on the lights.

The space was small, with a bedroom, bathroom, kitchenette, and living room. After years spent in monasteries and barracks, Travis loved having a place of his own. Grants and donations paid the bills and staff salaries for St. Dismas, while a few secretive patrons helped finance Travis's monster hunting. Travis had learned to live with little, but he was happy with the cozy space he had outfitted from thrift shops and yard sales.

"Better sit down before you fall down," he told Brent. "I'll get stuff to make up the couch for you." He grabbed sheets, a blanket, and a pillow and came back to find Brent half-asleep.

"Scoot over," he said, nudging Brent to one end of the sofa. "Then you can crash as hard as you want."

Brent muttered something unintelligible. Travis chuckled as he tucked the bedding into place and then gave Brent a gentle shove that sent him sprawling onto the cushions.

"Breakfast downstairs is pancakes and eggs," he said, tossing a blanket over Brent and pulling off his boots. "If you sleep through that, lunch is bologna sandwiches, chips, and carrots. I'll call Alex and let him know you're safe."

Alex Wilson, Brent's part-time assistant in his private investigator business, knew about the hunting side of Brent's life and was happy to cover absences. Travis and Brent had helped to save Alex and his husband from a dark witch, providing a rough introduction to the hidden world of the supernatural.

Thanks to the pain medication, Brent slept hard.

Travis wasn't as lucky.

His dreams stitched the worst memories together in a loop, picking the most terrifying moments, the most bitter losses. Travis relived monster fights he had barely survived, remembered exorcisms and possessions, smelled blood and tasted bile.

He woke from his own cries, sweating and heaving for breath. It took effort and long moments to slow his heartbeat and gather his wits.

That's in the past. I survived. I left the Sinistram. It's over. I'm alive.

Travis knew it would take a while for him to fall asleep again if that was even possible. Afraid he might have woken Brent, he padded out to check on his guest, relieved to find him breathing deeply and evenly, comfortable on the couch.

"Matthew gave you the good drugs," Travis muttered. He rarely minded not keeping whiskey in his quarters, but nights like this made him wish for a flask to blur the dreams and help him sleep.

With a sigh, Travis contented himself with a cup of chamomile tea before padding back to bed. The drink calmed his nerves, but he still tossed and turned and didn't drift off until it was nearly time for his alarm.

CHAPTER TWO

"I USED to have a spectacular night out before feeling this shitty." Brent stumbled to the small kitchen table, guided largely by the smell of fresh coffee. He still wore the clothing from the previous day, and his mouth tasted like roadkill.

"You're not in your twenties anymore. Getting older sucks." Travis put a steaming cup of coffee in front of Brent along with a plate of scrambled eggs and pancakes.

"Better than the alternative. Did you cook?"

Travis laughed. "No. I ran down and grabbed us breakfast plates from the dining hall. Figured I'd spare you having to get showered and dressed before you could eat."

Brent murmured his thanks, still a bit too drugged to be articulate. He took a gulp of hot coffee and bit back a moan of pleasure. Usually he hated losing his edge to medication, but Brent had gradually learned over the years to surrender to necessity. Refusing treatment only prolonged pain and extended his convalescence.

Travis took a seat across from him and dug into his stack of buttermilk pancakes and fluffy eggs. They ate in companionable silence. Travis refilled their coffee whenever the cups got low, and Brent reveled in the carb, caffeine, and protein fix topped off by the sugar hit of real maple syrup.

"Thanks for letting me crash."

Travis looked up. "I wasn't going to leave you on your own."

"I've survived before."

"You shouldn't have to. I could have been the one who got all beat up just as easily."

"Jon and Matthew take care of you," Brent said with his mouth full.

"We take care of each other," Travis replied.

Brent muttered something but didn't contradict him.

In the years since demons murdered his twin brother Danny and their parents, Brent had plunged into work—first in college, then the Army, the FBI, and a brief stint as a cop before becoming a private investigator and part-time monster hunter. He'd kept most people at a distance, afraid of getting them killed. Danny's ghost had kept him company for most of that time, but even he was gone now, possibly for good.

Once Brent and Travis had warily circled each other and decided against homicide, they'd developed a solid partnership and grudging friendship. Brent knew he still had plenty of shit to work through, but being accepted into Travis's circle with the St. Dismas crew provided the first sense of family he'd had in decades, and it surprised him how much that mattered.

"Have any intel on something new to hunt?" Brent asked after he'd cleaned his plate, swallowing the last of his coffee.

"Nothing solid. Probably wouldn't be a bad thing if we took the rest of the week off—heal up a little before we get thrown around again."

"Nah. I'll just be in the salt circle this time, and you can get tossed through the air." Brent smirked.

Travis pushed the bottles of pain medicine and muscle relaxants across the table. "Here you go. And if you try to 'forget' to take them, Alex will tell me."

"Turncoat," Brent whispered, although he didn't really mind having his friends watching out for him, even if it was something he still struggled to get used to.

"He just doesn't want to have to pick you up off the floor and haul your ass home—again," Travis pointed out, and Brent swore under his breath.

"That happened *once*," Brent argued.

"Apparently, it was memorable. Or traumatizing."

Brent stood, trying not to wince. "Seriously—I'm fine. I've been shot, stabbed, and worked over by the Mob. I'm going to go home, take a hot shower, check in with Alex, and then sleep the rest of the day. Okay?"

"Don't take the pills before you drive," Travis warned.

"Yes, Mother."

Travis flipped him off, but Brent could see that his friend's worry had eased.

"I'll call you when I get in. And if you want to check around dinner time to make sure I'm still breathing, that's fine," Brent added, knowing that Travis was truly concerned. It had been a long time since Brent had people who cared, and he was out of practice accepting their help.

"Okay. And if anything goes wrong, call," Travis said. "One of us will come pick you up."

"Yeah, yeah. Thanks for the grub. I appreciate it."

"That's what we're here for."

———

BRENT DID his best to hide how sore he was as he walked to his truck. He'd had much more serious injuries, but that didn't make his current situation any less painful.

He checked his rearview mirror as he drove, unable to shake the feeling that he was being followed. Despite not seeing any suspicious vehicles tailing him, Brent took a number of switchbacks and extra turns on his way home, just in case. When he pulled into the drive at his house and no other car closed in, he let out a long breath.

"Hello, Brent." The man stepped out from behind a hedge row. Brent's hand went immediately to his gun.

"No need for that," the stranger said.

"Oh, yeah? I'll be the judge of that," Brent challenged. The newcomer's dark suit plus his high-and-tight haircut gave Brent a good idea of who he was dealing with.

"You look a little worse for the wear," the man said, clucking his tongue. "Monster hunting not working out for you?"

"Go fuck yourself." Brent pulled his gun but kept it at his side—for now. "Why are you here?"

"Hoping you'll reconsider our offer," the man said. "Working for C.H.A.R.O.N. means you'll have the best of everything, plus support and backup. Legal protection. Cutting-edge weapons. The best intelligence network in the world—better than the CIA."

"No way in hell," Brent snapped. "Not going to happen."

"We can be patient," the stranger added. "Especially when there's an asset we find very valuable."

"I'm a *person*, not an *asset*. I've already been government property—Army and FBI. Done that. Not looking to re-up."

"Conscription is an option when national security is at risk." The agent's fake smile never faltered, but Brent could see steel in his eyes.

"Monster hunting is a dangerous business," Brent returned, equally cold. "People die before their time." If the agent wasn't stupid, he'd get the message.

"Like I said, we can be patient. Think about it." He sauntered away.

"No *fucking* way in hell!" Brent called after him before he turned and limped onto the porch.

Central Handling Arcane Relics and Occult Networks—otherwise known as C.H.A.R.O.N. —was one of several secret government organizations that dealt with aspects of the supernatural and paranormal. While some of the other groups focused on research, documentation, data gathering, and observation, Brent always thought CHARON's reputation for shady dealings and ruthlessness put it in movie villain territory.

After Brent's brush with demons in Iraq, CHARON took an interest in recruiting him, especially when they discovered that demons had killed his family and demonic activity had cropped up in his short stints with the FBI and police. Brent's time in the military and law enforcement left him wary, and he had no illusions that the CHARON agents were the good guys.

So far, he'd been able to elude their recruitment efforts.

Brent locked the door behind him and stripped off his clothing, feeling sore from head to toe. He grimaced as a glance in the mirror showed the full technicolor glory of the bruises that marked his skin.

Hot water made him groan as it loosened tight muscles and sluiced away the sweat and dirt of the fight. He lingered longer than necessary, enjoying a moment of quiet. All too soon, the water began to run cool, and he turned it off with reluctance, then toweled dry carefully. The loose sleep pants and oversized soft t-shirt felt good against his damaged skin.

Although Brent had promised to take his pills and go back to bed, he knew he needed to check on a few things first. Alex picked up on the first ring.

"Hey boss, you okay?" Alex sounded worried, and Brent appreciated his concern.

"Got thrown around a little, but nothing out of the ordinary."

"Travis seemed to think otherwise."

"Travis worries," Brent replied. "What's on my plate for today?"

"I already emailed you what I could and put a new folder in the shared drive with the documents that came in today. Nothing I can't handle. You can read everything that came in on the open cases if you feel up to it. I've got things covered," Alex assured him.

"Thanks," Brent said, grateful that he had an assistant and for off-duty hours, a phone service. Monster hunting didn't pay. It was more of a calling, or as Travis might put it, a process of atonement. No one took up hunting for the money. Behind every hunter lay a tragic story, someone they lost because they failed to save them. For Brent, that was his family, and he didn't think he could ever stop enough creatures or save enough people to balance the scales.

For the large percentage of his work that involved phone calls, internet searches, and reading documents, Brent worked from a home office. When he needed to meet with a client, Brent had an arrangement with a temporary office space company a few blocks away. Brent vetted their prospective clients, and in return he had use of one of their offices whenever he needed it.

Much of Alex's work, like Brent's, could be done remotely. When they needed to work together, Alex usually came to Brent's house, or collaborated via video call.

"I've got plenty to keep me busy. If you need anything—food, medicine, booze—just call me. I'm not far away."

"I'm okay, thanks," Brent replied, appreciating the offer. "I got a shower, and now I'm going to take my pain meds and pass out."

"Call if I can help. I don't mind."

"Thanks. I'm bruised, not bleeding out. I think I'll be okay."

Brent ended the call and stopped in the kitchen long enough to pour a glass of water to swallow his pills. He hobbled toward the bedroom.

"Hey, Danny," he said to the empty room. "You think I look bad? You should have seen the other guy." Brent knew his brother's ghost wasn't with him anymore, not since Danny had decided to play the hero on their last big case and sacrificed himself to seal away the evil spirits that had caused so much havoc and death. Still, Brent sometimes talked to him.

Can a ghost be destroyed? Is Danny gone for good? And if he couldn't come back to me, can he move on to somewhere better?

Brent had asked those questions in the months since Danny vanished, but was no closer to finding answers. Travis and other friends who were mediums had promised to help, but so far no one had made contact with his brother's spirit. Maybe they never would.

I'm not giving up. Brent swore. *I'm going to look for a way to bring you back.*

In the meantime, if speaking aloud like he had for years when he sensed Danny's ghost nearby gave him comfort, no one had to know.

"You'd have had a good laugh seeing me get thrown around like a rag doll. Not my proudest moment," he admitted, grateful that Travis hadn't ribbed him about it. "I don't fly well—big surprise."

He limped over to the bed and eased onto the mattress, biting back a groan as he lifted his legs to lie down. "Wish you were here, Bucko. I miss having you around. If you can hear me, get your ass back here. Or go hang out in heaven with Mom and Dad," he added, with a catch in his voice. "Just don't stay stuck."

Brent missed his brother's company and the telepathic communication they had perfected over the years. Even if Danny couldn't return, Brent swore he wouldn't leave him trapped with the dark spirits. "I'll get you out. I promise."

Weary in body and soul, Brent laid back and pulled the covers up. He felt the pain meds kicking in and gave himself up to their respite.

The distant ringing of a phone roused him. Groggy, Brent reached for the nightstand, and when he opened his eyes, he could tell from the angle of the sun that it was well past noon.

"What?" he answered without checking the caller ID, not awake enough for niceties.

"Brent Lawson?"

"Yeah. Who is this?"

"Brent. Thank God. It's Chris Horvath—and I need your help."

Brent wracked his foggy brain. *Horvath. Army. God, it's been years.*

"Chris? What's going on?" Brent sat up and swung his legs over the side of the bed, figuring he was done with sleep.

"You know things, right? About stuff that's supernatural? Like back in Iraq, when you saved your unit from that demon."

Brent felt like he'd been doused with cold water as Chris's words brought back bad memories. He switched the call to speaker and hit record. "Talk to me, Chris. What's happening?"

"People here are dying in really weird ways. Like something out of a horror movie. This has always been a hard-luck town, but the stuff that's happening now—it's not natural."

"Slow down, Chris. Give me a chance to catch up." Brent shambled to the kitchen and started a pot of coffee.

"I'm in a little burg called South Fork. It was a mining and railroad town before those went away," Chris said.

"You were from somewhere mid-state, weren't you?" His Army days were five years ago, but the memories were never far away, no matter how hard Brent tried to forget.

"Yeah. Here. Never intended to come back, but...well, that's another story. Just this week, it got crazy. People hacking themselves to pieces for no reason. Doc Medved says Becca got sliced up from the *inside*. People have seen killer shadows—"

"Okay." Brent scrubbed a hand down his face as he waited for the carafe to fill. "Give that to me again."

"Zeke Kendall hacked off his leg with a field knife. In pieces—starting with his foot and working his way up. No one knows why—he was alone at the time, but Zeke was a steady kind of guy. No drugs. Hell of a way to go," Chris said.

"Becca died in the parking lot where she worked. Doc Medved did the autopsy—said it looked like someone cut her with a scalpel internally."

"What about the 'killer shadows'?" Brent poured a cup of coffee before the brew cycle finished, desperate for caffeine.

"There have been stories about the shadows for a long time—I always thought they were urban legends. But now people say they see them right before something really bad happens and swear they've been chased by them. Several people have gone missing," Chris replied. "I grew up with these folks, Brent. I want to protect them, and I don't know how. All the weirdness reminded me of that time in Iraq, and I thought maybe you'd know how to stop what's going on."

I'm not Obi-Wan. But maybe I'm the closest thing he has.

One awful night during Brent's deployment, his team had gotten pinned down not by enemy fire, but by a demon. He'd recognized the signs, used what he had learned from movies and video games to keep the demon away, and saved his men. Now, after years hunting monsters, Brent knew a lot more—and Travis had even more sophisticated skills.

"Okay. I want to bring someone else into this with me—we work together. We'll drive out first thing in the morning. Text me your address. Is there somewhere we can stay?"

"The motel burned down, but I've got a couple of spare bedrooms. I'll send you the directions. Thank you, Brent. I'm at the end of my rope."

"See you in the morning." Brent ended the call and drank his coffee as he tried to make sense of Chris's story. *Vengeful ghosts? Maybe. Doesn't exactly sound like demons. Witches? Seems odd. Wonder what Travis will make of it? So much for "down time."*

Brent checked his watch and realized it was nearly suppertime. He searched the fridge, found a slice of leftover pizza, and washed it down with coffee. Then he collected his thoughts, snatched a cookie from the box on the table, and picked up his phone. He hit Travis's number on speed dial.

"Got plans for tomorrow? Because I think I've found a new case for us," he told Travis.

———

"AND AFTER ALL THIS TIME, Chris thought of you when he ran into something demonic?" Travis asked as they drove to South Fork.

"It was a pretty memorable story," Brent admitted. "We were all scared shitless—me most of all."

"But you got your people out alive, and you weren't afraid to use what you knew, no matter where you learned it," Travis countered. "Plenty of books and video games use legitimate occult sources for their raw material."

"It was all I had to go on," Brent said. "I've always thought that Danny's ghost was helping protect us, even though I didn't see him. I felt his presence plenty of times when we were in a jam over there." He sighed. "I miss him."

"He's not back yet?"

"You're the medium." Brent didn't mean to sound snappish, but between the fight with Oliver's ghost and their new worrisome case, he felt stretched thin.

"Newsflash—I don't sense every ghost in the whole world," Travis replied, sidestepping the tension. "Sometimes ghosts hide themselves. You're the expert on Danny."

"Do you think he'll come back?" Brent heard the wistfulness in his voice, but he knew Travis wouldn't judge him.

"I hope so, but there's no way to know for certain. If he's as stubborn as you are, I wouldn't put it past him to find a way," Travis answered. "It takes energy for ghosts to manifest. He might not have charged back up yet."

"Someone from CHARON showed up, trying to recruit me." Brent abruptly changed the subject. "When I got back from your place."

Travis raised an eyebrow. "And? Do I need to help you hide a body?"

Brent gave a dry chuckle. "I thought about it. He wasn't worth the effort. I told him to fuck off. He made some vague threats, and I let him know that wouldn't work. I suspect someone will come by again sooner or later. They don't give up."

"Same with the Sinistram. If they think they're going to outwait me, they'll be disappointed," Travis said, resolve clear in his voice.

"I did give Chuck Pettis a call." Brent tried to get comfortable on the Crown Vic's big front bench seat. "Asked if he'd heard any

CHARON chatter in his circles. He hadn't, but he said he'd keep an ear out. I don't like them sniffing around."

The most direct way to South Fork was State Route 22, a secondary highway that wound through small towns and stretches of forest. The natural beauty of the hills and valleys offset the unmistakable evidence that the area's best days were long ago.

Coal had been king here a hundred years ago, shaft mines, not the strip mining common in later decades. Railroads carried coal and timber through the valleys, and passengers too for a while.

But the mines closed, the logging companies moved on, and the trains stopped coming. People left. Those who remained either had nowhere to go or stayed out of loyalty to place or family. *Chris probably fell into that category*, Brent thought, vaguely remembering that he had mentioned aging family in town.

"How are you feeling?" Travis had waited half an hour into their drive to ask, and Brent gave his partner credit for patience.

"Better than yesterday. Functional." Brent still ached, but he had put up with much worse in the Army. Ibuprofen could handle the pain at this point, although he wasn't sure how stiff he'd be after their car ride.

"Did your sources find out anything about the kinds of deaths Chris mentioned?" Brent asked.

Travis shook his head without taking his eyes off the road. "I've got people looking into it, but nothing solid yet. The details don't quite fit with vengeful spirits, but I'm not quite sure what else they might be—or what could cause that sort of damage. To tell you the truth, it worries me."

"Guess we need to wait and see what Chris has for us. He was very levelheaded, so if something spooked him enough to call me after all this time, it's probably worse than he let on."

They drove across the bridge into town as rain fell in a steady downpour.

"Look." Brent pointed at a faded sign painted on the wall of a building. It might once have read "Welcome to South Fork," but now the most legible word was just "South." "A sign you can see from a bridge that says 'South'—that's what Darius warned us about."

"Shit. You're right. The other side looks pretty normal to me," Travis said. "I guess they moved hell—at least for now."

The gray sky didn't improve the appearance of the area, highlighting the general state of decline. Most houses were in need of paint and repair. Few stores remained open on Main Street. Vacant shops or empty spaces where buildings had been torn down were more common. The cars parked at the curb were older models, and the one restaurant—a diner—appeared to have been built in the fifties.

"Gloomy place," Travis observed. "What does Chris do for a living?"

"He runs Fisher's." Brent directed Travis through several turns to the other side of the small town where they parked in front of a cement block building.

"I guess this is Fisher's," Brent said. Potholes dotted the gravel parking lot, full from the recent rain. Still, the fresh paint on the walls and sign suggested that of all the places in South Fork, the tavern was the most prosperous.

"Not sure how Chris ended up running a bar here," Brent said. "When I knew him, he wanted to move to the city and never come back."

"People change," Travis replied with a shrug. "Look at us."

They parked close to the door. Brent hesitated, frowning as he scanned the lot.

"What?"

Brent shook his head. "Nothing. I thought I saw something move over there. I have the feeling we're being watched."

"If we are, we'll figure out who and why. One step at a time," Travis replied. "First, let's try to get inside without drowning." They ran from the car to the door through the pouring rain.

Fisher's interior was cozy, clearly a local gathering place. While the paneled walls, dropped ceiling, and tiled floor showed wear, the bar looked clean, and the food smelled delicious. Bowling trophies lined shelves along one wall. A large frame on another wall beneath the taxidermied head of an antlered buck held engraved nameplates for decades of prize-winning hunts. Signed, faded photos of long-ago notables covered the wall behind the cash register.

Sports jerseys and pennants for the local high school, community colleges, and nearby universities showed civic pride. Brent gave Chris credit for making Fisher's a town hub in a place that desperately needed soul and solidarity.

Although it was barely noon, a few older men sat together at the bar, nursing coffee instead of beer. A widescreen over the bar played ESPN. The aromas suggested burgers and fries and perhaps spaghetti. Brent's stomach growled.

"Go ahead and seat yourselves." A woman looked up from the cash register at the end of the bar. "We'll get right to you."

Brent cleared his throat. "I'm looking for Chris Horvath."

"He's busy in the back—" she began.

"I've got this. Thanks, Katy." Chris appeared in the doorway at the end of the bar. Although years had passed, Brent would have recognized him anywhere. A bit grayer, a few more lines around the corners of his eyes, softer in the belly, but still definitely the same man Brent had served with half a world away.

"Captain Lawson!" Chris strode toward them with a broad smile. He shook hands with Brent and then did the same with Travis.

"Just Brent," he corrected. "I haven't been a captain for a long time."

"Old habits," Chris laughed.

"This is Travis Dominick. We work together," Brent told him. "And we're hoping that we can lend a hand."

Chris's smile faded. "I hope so too." He motioned for them to follow him to a booth in the far corner. "What would you like to eat? Lunch is on me."

"A Coke and a burger would be great, thanks," Brent said, and

Travis seconded the request. Chris walked to the bar to place the order, leaving them alone.

"What you expected?" Travis asked under his breath.

"Wasn't sure what I thought we'd find," Brent replied. "That's Chris for sure, a little worse for the wear. Something's spooked him bad. Chris was unflappable. If he's rattled, there's a good reason."

CHAPTER THREE

CHRIS RETURNED and pulled a chair up to the end of the table so he could see both Brent and Travis. "Thanks for coming; I know South Fork is out of the way."

Brent shrugged. "We go where the work is. You had quite a story when you called me. Want to start from the beginning?"

Chris sighed and ran his hands over his face and into his hair. "You're going to think I'm crazy."

"Try us." Travis got a gut feeling that Chris was a good man at the end of his rope. That squared with the memories Brent had shared.

"South Fork has always been a hard-luck town. Nothing good ever seemed to sink roots here," Chris replied. "The farming was hardscrabble at best. The mines and the little bit of manufacturing we had were dangerous. So were logging and the railroads. Something about this land seems to want to break people."

Sodas were delivered to the table, then Chris continued.

"For a while, we got enough traffic from the highway to keep a few hotels and restaurants running, but when they put in the new interstates, that took away most of the travelers. Hell, the local hospital is going to be shut down in a couple of months." He managed a bitter smile. "This here's what you call a 'Springsteen kind of town,' the sort the Boss sings about. A dead end for dead-enders."

"Why'd you come back? How come people stay?" Brent asked.

"I came back because I didn't have anywhere else to go," Chris said. "Going into the Army was better than having my Mom's boyfriend-of-the-week slap me around. Got married—it didn't last. Drifted around, finally came back to South Fork, and got a job here at the bar. Mr. Fisher's grandfather founded the place. His son was my best friend in high school who wasn't lucky enough to come back from Iraq. When Mr. Fisher found out he had terminal cancer, he left the bar to me—said I was the only 'son' he had left. And here I am."

Chris paused, looking around the bar as if taking it in with fresh eyes. "Thing about being a bartender—I know all the dirt, the skeletons in the closets, the dirty secrets. And I'm too tired to care. Takes me a couple of breaths every morning to convince myself to get out of bed, and I'm only thirty-seven. I figure running this joint is my atonement for all the times I've fucked up. Fisher's might be the one good thing holding this town together. It's a community hub, a house of refuge, and a confessional. Especially since old Father Prochazka crawled into the sacramental wine and never came out."

Travis winced, remembering too many older priests he'd known over the years who had done the same. The priesthood was a tough gig when times were going well. It was impossible to avoid being sucked into the abyss of human suffering when bad times hit.

"Truth is, no one's been answering prayers from South Fork for a long time," Chris added.

A server brought their meals and a pot of coffee. They were silent as they ate, wolfing down the food, but lingering over the java when she returned to take their plates.

"Tell us about the weird stuff," Travis urged. "I promise we'll believe you."

Chris took a drink, and Travis guessed the man was buying himself time to think.

"Zeke Kendall was closing up over at the farm machinery shop—just him and Tim Landon were still around. Tim said Zeke had been fine all day. Then when they were just about to lock up, Zeke's bad leg started bothering him. He got hurt in a tractor accident years ago, and between that and his diabetes, his leg hasn't been right ever since."

Chris stared into his cup. "Tim says that Zeke started kicking like something crawled up his pant leg, hopping around, stomping on the floor like he was stepping on bugs. Tim went to see what was wrong, but then Zeke grabbed a field knife and swung for his own ankle. Tim tried to grab his arm, but Zeke probably outweighed that kid by fifty pounds. Zeke knocked him out of the way and hacked his foot clean off."

Brent flinched. Travis took a deep breath to keep his lunch down.

"Tim says he went after Zeke again, and before he could stop him, Zeke tried to chop off his leg above the knee. Tim ran for the front to call 911. Zeke bled out before they got there."

"Fuck," Brent muttered. "Was he tripping? Did he have mental health issues?"

Chris shrugged. "Drugs? No. Zeke never even smoked cigarettes. As for having issues, no more than anyone else in town, I'd wager."

"Did Zeke say anything while all this was going on?" Travis asked. "You said he was stomping around—hallucination?"

"That was Tim's guess. He thought he heard Zeke say something about 'maggots,' but when Doc Medved looked at the body, there wasn't any gangrene, no infection. Definitely no maggots."

"Did anyone have a grudge against Zeke? Enough to put a curse on him?" Travis wasn't sure how Chris would react, but a suggestion that spells might be involved was one of the saner alternatives.

"Zeke? Not that I ever heard—and I hear most things, sooner or later," Chris replied. "He was a real straight arrow. Kept his head down, did his work. His wife died from breast cancer a few years back, kids left town. Just him and his dog. Tim adopted Buster since Zeke didn't have family close by."

"And until the...incident...nothing seemed off about Zeke?" Brent probed.

"Not according to Tim," Chris countered. "Zeke hadn't been sick, hadn't been drinking, just going about his business like normal. Until he wasn't."

Brent swallowed hard, and Travis figured his partner was fighting the urge to puke. "You said there was someone else who died under strange circumstances?"

Chris snorted. "More than one, but these are the most recent. The deaths are always gruesome, but there's less time between them now."

"Is there some sort of historical anniversary—" Travis began, but Chris shook his head.

"Not that we can find. We looked when the sane explanations didn't cover things anymore." He drained his coffee cup. "Becca Thompson worked over at the diner. She was walking out to her car after her shift with Sherri Carson. Sherri said Becca got twitchy and thought she saw something around the edge of the parking lot, but Sherri didn't see anything."

"Then Becca started screaming and clutching her belly. Sherri says it looked like there was a hand inside Becca's body, moving around. Becca went down choking on blood, and she was dead before Sherri got 911 on the line. The coroner said something carved her up *from the inside*," Chris said.

"But whatever it was left Sherri alone?" Travis frowned, trying to make Chris's story match up with the lore.

"Poor girl's a total basket case after what she saw, but the *thing* that got Becca didn't hurt Sherri," Chris replied.

"Is there any way we can get a look at the bodies and the places the deaths occurred?" Brent asked. "We might be able to pick up on something that didn't stand out to people who haven't run across the occult before."

"I figured you'd say that. Already told Tony Calabrese—he's our sheriff—that I was calling in some favors to try to figure out what the hell is going on. Tony's good people—and not too proud to ask for help. Plus, he's a local boy. Probably knows everyone in town a whole lot better than he'd like to. He can take you over to the morgue and get Doc Medved to let you in."

"Thanks," Brent replied. "That's a good starting point."

"You said Becca thought she saw something in the shadows," Travis said. "Did Sherri see it? We thought we glimpsed a shape on our way in but didn't get a good look."

Chris sighed. "That's what the kids call 'sneaks' and grown-ups call 'devil dogs.' You know what this end of Pennsylvania is like—lots of Eastern Europeans like my family who brought their lore with them. There are old Slavic stories my grandma used to tell about creatures that hunt people. When folks go missing, and we can't find the body, people say the shadow dogs got them."

"What do you think they are?" Brent asked.

"No idea—but I think they're real. I don't know where they come from or why they've shown up now, but no one goes wandering around after dark lately unless they've got a death wish," Chris told them.

Chris made a call and then looked up. "Tony'll be here in about ten minutes, and he'll take you over to the hospital. Said he'd get Doc primed to expect you. Come back here when you're done, and I'll try to answer whatever questions Tony didn't."

Right on time, a stocky blond man in his late thirties wearing a sheriff's jacket walked into the bar. Several of the patrons greeted him by name or title, and Calabrese either waved or called back to them. He scanned the room and then made his way over to Travis and Brent. *Guess it's not hard to tell we're not from around here.*

"I'm Tony Calabrese—South Fork's sheriff. You must be Chris's friends from Pittsburgh."

Brent shook his hand. "Brent Lawson. Served with Chris."

"Travis Dominick. Brent and I work together." Travis liked the sheriff's firm handshake.

"Chris and I grew up together," Calabrese said. "Shipped out together but didn't end up going to the same places." He headed for the door and gestured for them to follow. "C'mon. Doc's waiting. Don't blame me if you lose your lunch."

Brent rode in the front seat of the sheriff's Jeep, and Travis climbed in the back.

"I know you served with Chris, but I get a whiff of law enforcement from you," Calabrese said as they drove.

"Did a stint with the FBI. Spent some time as a cop. Now, the day job is private investigator," Brent replied.

Calabrese eyed Travis in the mirror. "You're not a cop. Not sure what you are."

"Ex-priest," Travis replied smoothly. "Did some monster hunting for the Vatican. Now, I'm freelance." The short version was true—and left out a whole lot of complications.

"Huh. I thought that kind of stuff just happened in the movies," Calabrese replied, accepting the explanation without quibbling. "Well, I sure hope you know more than we do because it's been a shitshow around here—and that's saying something."

He stopped in front of a brick building. The central rectangle looked like it dated from the early 1900s. The architecture of newer wings suggested they might have been added in the 1950s and 1970s. Travis remembered that Chris said the hospital would be closing soon and wondered what would take its place.

"Here—take these," Calabrese said, handing off two rain slickers marked "Sheriff's Department." They'll keep you from getting soaked, and it'll cut off a lot of questions when you go poking around. I don't want to keep getting calls to go arrest you."

"Much obliged," Brent said.

Just as Calabrese opened his door, an alert blared on his phone. He checked the device and swore under his breath. "Storm warning. Guess we're supposed to get a bunch of bad thunderstorms. Like we haven't had too damn much rain lately already."

He pocketed his phone and led the way into the hospital, sparing a wave for the security officer at the front desk before leading Travis and Brent down a corridor to a staircase and into the basement.

Calabrese stopped in front of the door to the morgue. "I'm guessing this isn't your first time? You've seen autopsies before?"

Travis appreciated the consideration but knew they had seen far worse. "We'll be okay."

Calabrese knocked and then entered. "Hey, Doc? Brought you those tourists I told you about."

Doc Medved came out of the back, still wearing scrubs and a surgical apron. He looked to be in his mid-fifties with a full head of curly graying hair and a square face with intelligent, dark eyes. He gave Travis and Brent the once-over and then nodded curtly.

"Gentlemen. Sheriff Tony says you're here to help. If Chris vouches for you, I'm good with that." He held out booties, gloves, and masks. "Suit up, and follow me."

Travis hated the smell of hospitals, and morgues were worse. He'd never been squeamish, a blessing in this line of work, but the knowledge that the pale corpse laid out on the slab had, just days before, been going about life weighed heavily on him.

"We've heard some tall tales," Brent said as they approached the two most recent bodies. "Can you substantiate?"

Medved gestured toward the opened drawers. "See for yourselves."

Zeke Kendall had the build and beard of a lumberjack. Broad shoulders, strong arms, and long legs made him a man-mountain, and calloused hands attested to years of hard work. Travis swallowed hard at the protruding bone and ragged flesh ending his right leg above the ankle and the deep gashes that tore into the meat of his thigh.

"Zeke was a good man," Medved said, shaking his head. "He deserved better. They all did."

"The witness seemed to think Kendall thought there was something wrong with his leg." Brent moved closer for a better look.

"Zeke had some nerve damage in his leg, various causes," Medved confirmed. "That could cause numbness or tingling. Some people say it can feel like ants crawling, but it wasn't anything new for Zeke. All that had been going on for a couple of years. He knew what it felt like and what it was. No reason to freak out and try to chop his whole damn leg off."

"And the other one?" Travis asked, looking at the woman's body on the next table. His eyes widened at the vicious slashes on her abdomen—all of them straight and clean like from a scalpel.

"Becca Thompson. Nice lady. Didn't know her well—glad about that now. Carved up from the *inside*. Something shredded her insides and cut its way out, but it didn't use claws or teeth. The cuts are thin and clean, like a knife or a scalpel. Damned if I know what does that, but the evidence is clear," Medved told them.

Medved and Calabrese stepped aside, giving Travis and Brent a chance to take a closer look at the bodies. Travis suspected the two might have a bet on whether he and Brent would puke, but if so, they'd be disappointed. The demons they'd hunted left their possessed victims in much worse shape.

Travis wondered if his detachment meant he'd lost some of his humanity and figured he didn't want to know the answer to that question.

"The angle should have been all wrong," Brent murmured, looking at the stump of Kendall's do-it-yourself amputation. "Should have been hard for him to get momentum behind his swing to cut through on the first go."

"You think he was possessed?" Travis mused. "Or ridden by something?"

"My gut says 'no' to demons and 'maybe' to some other kind of entity," Brent replied. They spoke quietly, not yet ready to share their thoughts with the others.

"Different methods of killing, victims weren't in the same place," Travis noted. "Demons usually do what they do for a reason—at least, one that makes sense to them. We don't have enough pieces of the puzzle to figure out the 'why' yet."

"You got the storm warning?" Medved asked Calabrese as Travis and Brent snapped photos with their phones and made sure they had viewed the injuries from all angles.

"Just what we don't need," Calabrese muttered. "High winds too. Pete Carmody went out to the reservoir to check the levels. All this rain—it damn well better hold."

"Been there for seventy years," Medved replied. "Not the first time we've had downpours."

Calabrese shrugged, looking antsy. "Yeah. I know. I can't shake the feeling that things are gonna get worse."

Medved slapped him on the back. "That's what we pay you for, Tony. Your job is to worry about everything so the rest of us can keep on keeping on."

Calabrese's phone rang with a different tone, and Travis looked up in time to see the sheriff's expression as he spoke to the caller. For just an instant, Calabrese's face registered shock and pain before his professional mask slipped into place.

"I'm downstairs in the morgue. We'll be right up." He looked up. "Got another self-mutilation case; only this one got stopped before it turned fatal."

"Fuck," Medved murmured. "Who?"

"Rick Donaldson," Calabrese answered. "He's smashed up but not dead. Paul Sullivan brought him in, says he saw it happen. Better go find out the details." A glance summoned Travis and Brent to accompany him. "I'll let you know if we find out anything to explain what's going on," he told Medved before they headed back upstairs.

Travis and Brent trailed the sheriff as he took the stairs two at a time, then strode down the corridor toward the Emergency Room. No one asked Calabrese for ID, and since they traveled in his wake, no one stopped them, either.

The sheriff paused just inside the doors to the main treatment area. "Where's Rick Donaldson?" he asked the first nurse who came close enough to question.

"I'll get Dr. Thompkins," she said, barely breaking stride.

Several minutes later, a dark-haired woman in a blood-spattered white coat emerged from behind the privacy curtains. "Hello, Sheriff. I've got to say you're Johnny-on-the-spot tonight."

Calabrese managed a wan smile. "Hi, Donna. How's Rick?"

Thompkins's polite smile faded. "He's a mess. Something large and heavy shattered his right shoulder, his left thigh bone, pelvis, his left arm at the elbow, and several ribs. Rick's lucky to be alive. He's under heavy sedation for the pain."

"*Something?*" Calabrese probed.

Thompkins sighed. "We're still trying to confirm the story Paul Sullivan gave when he brought Rick in." She glanced behind her. "Look, I need to get back to Rick. Get a coffee and come back in half an hour. I might know more then."

She disappeared behind the curtain, and Calabrese motioned for them to follow him back to the ER entrance. "The coffee here is pretty good for a hospital. And the pie is made over at the bake shop in town. Not a bad place to wait, all things considered."

When they reached the hospital cafeteria, Calabrese stopped so abruptly that Travis nearly ran into him.

"That's Paul Sullivan." Calabrese nodded to a man who sat alone at a table out of the main traffic flow. "The guy who brought Rick to the hospital. Let's get coffee and join him. Rick is going to be too drugged up to answer questions, and Donna—Dr. Thompkins—can tell us about his injuries, but probably not how he got them."

Travis felt pleasantly surprised at how good the blackberry pie looked, and the coffee smelled much better than he expected. He and Brent followed Calabrese when he headed to where Sullivan sat. Everything about the man's body language made it clear he didn't want to be bothered.

"Hello, Paul. Can we join you?" Calabrese phrased it as a request, but given the circumstances, Sullivan had to realize his options were limited.

"Be my guest." Sullivan didn't look up, but he twitched his hand toward the empty chairs.

"These are friends of Chris's—Travis Dominick and Brent

Lawson," Calabrese said. "They came in from Pittsburgh to lend a hand." He paused. "I'm sorry about Rick."

Sullivan shivered and seemed to close in on himself. "Yeah. Me too."

"Dr. Thompkins said you brought him in. He's not going to be able to tell us anything for a while," Calabrese said. "So I thought maybe you could tell me what happened."

Paul stared down at his cup for a moment, long enough that Travis wondered whether he would answer.

"Rick and I were playing cards when all of a sudden his hunting dogs started to howl. They'd been quiet all night, so he figured there was a bear or some such riling them," Sullivan said quietly. "Told me to stay inside, and he grabbed his shotgun. I figured he'd shoot off a few rounds and scare whatever it was away, and we'd go back to the game."

Sullivan toyed with his spoon. "I went to the window, but I couldn't see anything out there. Rick started yelling, and it wasn't like he was shouting at an animal. It sounded like he saw something. I figured there might be trouble, so I grabbed one of the fireplace tools and went out onto the porch."

Travis felt sure that whatever Sullivan had seen spooked him badly.

"There was a man, but he was dressed wrong—like he was from a long time ago. He had a sledgehammer in his hands. Rick shot at him, but he must have missed. Then the guy starts swinging the sledge-hammer at Rick, and I knew he was going to kill him if I didn't do something. So I ran out and swung the fireplace poker at him and..."

"He disappeared?" Travis supplied, having a feeling where this was heading.

Paul's gaze snapped up. "You're humoring me."

Travis shook his head. "Not at all. The fireplace tool was likely made of iron. When you hit the ghost, the iron dispelled him."

"Ghost?" Paul looked as if he was desperate to assure himself that he hadn't gone mad.

"What did the man look like?" Brent asked, leaning forward. "Can you describe his clothing?"

Paul drew a deep breath, and his gaze shifted focus as if he was examining his memory. "He had an old-fashioned shirt with a funny collar and loose trousers with suspenders. Looked like someone from those old-timey photographs, with deep-set eyes and longish hair and a hillbilly beard."

"And he had a sledgehammer?" Calabrese confirmed.

Sullivan nodded. "It vanished when he did. Looked hard-used."

His voice dropped to nearly a whisper. "Rick was screaming, pleading for mercy, but the man didn't stop until I chased him away."

"Did the ghost come back?" Calabrese asked.

"No. I called 911 and stayed with Rick until the ambulance came. He was in bad shape. I was afraid he wouldn't make it."

"You saved his life," Travis said. "His shotgun didn't work because he either missed the ghost or wasn't firing iron pellets. If the ghost hadn't been interrupted, he'd have finished the job."

"Scared the shit out of me," Sullivan admitted. "But I wasn't going to let Rick get smashed to death."

Calabrese checked his watch. "Dr. Thompkins said to come back in half an hour. How about we all finish our food and then go talk to her."

When they returned to the Emergency Room, a nurse was watching for them and went to bring Thompkins. The doctor gestured for them to follow her into a consultation room.

"I can speak to the sheriff because he's law enforcement," she told them. "If he vouches for the rest of you, I'll let you hash it out with HIPAA if there's a problem." Thompkins leaned against the wall while the others sat around the small table.

"Rick's still in surgery. His injuries are severe, and it's going to take pins and plates to put him together again. He'll probably always have a limp—if he is able to walk again. Once he's out of surgery, he'll be heavily sedated. We'll bring him out of sedation as his pain level wanes. That could take a few days," Thompkins told them.

Talking to Rick wasn't likely to be possible any time soon, Travis realized, not in time to ward off whatever was causing South Fork's gruesome streak of deaths.

"Thank you," Calabrese replied. "When he does wake up, please make sure someone notifies me. I don't know what he'll remember, but his testimony could be important."

"What kind of sick fucker does that to someone?" Thompkins asked, looking to Calabrese as if he had the answer.

"I don't know, Donna. But we're going to find out," the sheriff reassured her.

Travis didn't add that the culprit was likely long dead and beyond the reach of the law. "Let's go back to Fisher's. I've got questions."

CHAPTER FOUR

"THERE'S A LOT TO UNPACK," Brent said as they walked to the sheriff's Jeep. "Is there somewhere we can go to talk?"

Calabrese chuckled. "Sure. There's the diner, Fisher's, and the processing room at my office. Take your pick."

"Fisher's," Brent replied. "Quieter than the diner, and I'm allergic to jails."

"Suit yourself—although once Fisher's opens in the morning, it's hardly ever empty. People drift in and out all day," the sheriff said.

They drove back to the bar as a light rain fell. True to Calabrese's prediction, three cars were parked in front of Fisher's despite it being past time for lunch. Chris looked up when they entered and jerked his head toward a table in the far corner. Brent saw a hand-lettered "Reserved" sign claiming it for them.

"Guess we've got a space for the duration," Brent said as he took the far chair on the right side. Travis took the seat next to him, putting Calabrese across from them.

"What did you want to know?" the sheriff asked. "I've got to get back to the office before too long."

"Is there any significance behind the way the people are dying?" Travis asked. "The circumstances are pretty unusual."

"Not to my recollection, and I grew up here as well as being sheriff for the last few years," Calabrese replied. "My wife Tammy works at the library—they've got a lot of historical archives, assuming that sort of thing would be recorded."

"It's a start," Travis said, making a note on his phone.

"The people who died—were they in some sort of trouble?" Brent pressed. "Owed money, abusive partner, cooking meth...that sort of thing?"

Calabrese shook his head. "Nobody's a saint, but I'm not sure any of those three even had recent parking tickets. No warrants served, no prior arrests, no history of altercations. Folks around here don't have the energy for a whole lot of drama because putting one foot in front of another takes damn near everything you've got."

"Did any of them have a sudden streak of exceptionally good luck?" Travis asked, and Brent knew his partner was looking for demon deals.

Calabrese laughed. "In South Fork? If they had, they'd have high-tailed it out of town. Nah. More like the opposite. Zeke Kendall put a new engine in his truck last week that was gonna have him working extra shifts until Kingdom Come. Becca's divorce just became final. I drove her asshole of an ex to the edge of town myself and told him to never come back. Rick just got a good job with the county road crew —that he's not going to be able to do with the way he got busted up."

So much for demon deals come due.

Chris sauntered to the table with four cups and a pot of coffee and took a seat at the table. "Coffee's on the house. Did you see what you needed to see?"

"Saw it—still figuring out what to make of what we saw," Brent replied. "Can you give us a rough map of where the attacks happened? Maybe if we go to the sites, we'll pick up on something."

Chris flipped the paper placemat over and pulled a pen from the order pad in his bar apron. He drew the main streets of South Fork with boxes to indicate landmarks. "Here's the feed store where Zeke Kendall died. And the diner where Becca was attacked. And Rick's trailer," he said, adding an "X" for each one. "Tony's crew has been over all of them, and with the rain, anything that got left behind is probably ruined, but fresh eyes can't hurt."

"We aren't doubting that you're thorough," Travis said, with a look directed at Calabrese. "But supernatural entities can leave behind traces that might not look like normal clues."

"Have at it," Calabrese said. "Hell, if you can stop people from dying, I'll give you a fucking ticker tape parade."

"If you don't mind me asking, I overheard you and the coroner talking about someone checking a dam?" Travis put in.

Calabrese sighed. "Yeah. About that. South Fork is downriver from an earthen dam. It's held for almost a century, but that means every year the parts are a little older. Pete's one of our city engineers, and he keeps an eye on it because of the water supply. With all the rain, we're a bit twitchy. It'll take him a while to check things over. I'd like to know it's in good shape before this next storm front rolls through."

"There's a chance it might not be?" Brent exchanged a look with Travis.

"You ever hear of the Johnstown Flood?" Calabrese replied. "It was the *old* South Fork Dam that failed. Killed fifteen hundred people and leveled a city. That was a hundred and thirty-some years ago. It would be 'South Fork luck' to get a repeat performance."

"South Fork luck?" Travis raised an eyebrow. Brent remembered Chris using a similar expression.

"Crime isn't a big problem—people in these parts don't have much worth stealing," Calabrese replied, pausing to drain his coffee cup. "I've got a deputy and an office manager. We stay too busy documenting 'accidents' and suicides. Haven't seen this much carnage since Afghanistan. I'm probably crazy not to pull up stakes and leave. But I love my wife and my kids—and my friends. So I'm gonna dig in my heels and fight to keep what's ours."

The sheriff checked his watch. "Gotta go. Here's my number." He pulled a card from his pocket. "Call if you find anything. I'll swing back through around dinner time to see how your day went."

Brent sipped his cooling coffee and watched the sheriff leave. "Seems like a good guy. Law enforcement types don't usually make us feel real welcome."

"Tony's solid," Chris replied. "It didn't hurt that I vouched for you and that the three of us were in the war. South Fork ain't much, but it's home." He paused. "When you're ready to call it a day, let me know. I've got two spare bedrooms if you're not too choosy. I'll even spot you cold cereal or toast and jelly for breakfast. And the price is right."

"Thank you," Brent said after gaining a confirming nod from Travis. "That would be great."

Chris gave a tired smile. "You hauled ass out here when I asked for help. It's the least I can do."

Brent finished his coffee and set the cup aside, and Travis did the same and stood. "We'd better go do our exploring before it starts raining any harder. Anything else we should look at while we're out there?"

Chris shook his head. "South Fork looks like every other one-stop-light town you've ever driven through. If you're interested, the Protestant cemetery is on the east end, and the Catholic one is on the west end. Don't get adventurous around the old coal tipple or what's left of the Leigh Mine over on Route 3. The mine's boarded up for good reason—cave-ins and bad air. The tipple and the rest of the processing plant is likely to fall over in a hard wind."

"Sounds like our kind of place," Travis remarked with a wry smile.

"That's why I'm warning you. I'm sure there are ghosts. There were plenty of deaths back in the day, most of them gruesome. But nothing lately. We don't want you two added to the toll—need you alive if you're going to save our skins," Chris said.

Brent snapped a mock salute, and Chris flipped him off. "Message received."

"You always were a smart-ass son of a bitch," Chris muttered.

The slow, steady rain promised to soak everything, coming down harder than before.

"Thoughts?" Brent asked as Travis drove. This was the first chance they'd had to talk privately since they arrived in town, and he wondered if they had the same questions and noted similar details.

"I think your friend Chris and the sheriff are straight shooters," Travis replied. "For once, there's a sheriff who doesn't seem to resent us—which tells me that whatever's going on scares him. He wants to do right by his town, even if it means asking outsiders for help. I respect that."

Holding to the slow speed limit gave them a chance to get a good look at South Fork. A brick Methodist church and a large cemetery anchored one end, giving way to a one-street downtown. Most of the buildings along that stretch dated from the 1920s; none looked newer than the 1960s. Several were boarded up. A few vacant lots between the shops attested to fires or demolition. The only person in sight was an old man trudging along with a brightly colored grocery bag.

"The hardware store looks like a general purpose sort of place," Brent observed. "There's a diner, school, hospital, grocery store, sheriff's office, hair salon, dollar discount. Hell, I don't even remember passing a Walmart on our way in. Can people shop online? Do they have to find a mall?"

Travis snickered. "You sound like a spoiled city boy."

"I *am* a spoiled city boy," Brent countered.

"I get the feeling folks here keep things pretty basic," Travis replied. "Most young adults likely skipped town long ago, and for the ones who stayed, their kids will fly the coop as soon as they can."

A local pharmacy, offices for doctors, a dentist, a lawyer, and an insurance agent rounded out the main drag, along with a long-defunct movie theater and a fire hall. Anchoring the other end of town was a bowling alley, the Our Lady of Tribulation Catholic Church with its own cemetery next door, and finally, the feed store.

"Not much of a selling point that the only way to leave town in either direction is past a cemetery," Brent said. The overcast sky and steady rain dimmed his mood, already uneasy after what they had seen at the morgue and heard from Chris and Calabrese. What remained of South Fork gave credence to the description of the town as "hard luck."

A scream sounded, close by, shrill enough that they could hear it through the closed car windows. Travis pulled to the side, and they jumped out, guns drawn at their sides, looking for danger.

Brent glanced back the way they came. "Shit. Where's that old man?"

Ignoring the rain, Brent and Travis ran back to where they had last seen him. Travis pointed to an alley, and they headed into it with Travis taking point.

Brent spotted the colorful shopping bag the old man had been carrying lying in a puddle next to a dumpster. A streak of fresh blood marred its bright design.

"Over there," Travis whispered, pointing farther down the alley to a creature that resembled a tall wolf but with a prickly line of hair down its spine like a hyena and a large, lantern-jawed head.

They opened fire. The wolf creature howled and dodged behind a dumpster. By the time they cautiously closed in on the location, the beast was gone.

They searched but found no trace of the old man other than his discarded bag.

"Where the hell is the old guy?" Brent fretted. "He's got to be nearby. That thing didn't have time to go far."

They checked the dumpsters, stairwells, and doorways to no avail.

"It must have carried the man off when it ran, but I've got no idea how or where," Travis admitted. "Then again, if this is its hunting ground, it knows the area a lot better than we do."

Brent called Calabrese and told him everything they had seen. He promised to send his deputy and acknowledged that his team was unlikely to find anything if Travis and Brent had already scoured the area.

"We'll watch for any missing person reports," the sheriff said. "Then again, a lot of our seniors in town live alone, so sad as it is to say this, no one might notice for a while. Keep me posted if you see anything else."

They headed back to the Crown Vic, even more rain-soaked than before.

"Are you picking up on any spirits?"

Travis paused as if searching with his senses. "I haven't seen any ghosts yet, but I can feel their presence. Maybe they're keeping some distance to figure us out. I don't feel threatened, but there are more here than in most places. That makes me wonder why they haven't moved on."

"The living certainly have," Brent remarked. "Not a lot of people out and about or cars parked. It's a crummy day, but usually folks still have errands to run. Maybe people are thinking twice about going out unless they absolutely have to."

"How about you? Getting anything on your 'demon radar'?"

Brent shook his head, knowing Travis was really asking for his gut feeling since he didn't have any special psychic abilities. "Nothing yet —although there's some sort of low-level resonance, like static in the background or music that's too quiet to really hear. It's there—I just can't make it out. And I keep seeing movement in the shadows out of the corner of my eye, but nothing's ever there."

"Let's see if those impressions get stronger near the sites of the attacks," Travis said. "Then I'm thinking that maybe we should go to the library and see if the sheriff's wife can pull up some town history."

"You've got a theory?" Brent enjoyed hearing how Travis's mind worked. Brent approached problems from a military and law enforce-ment perspective, while Travis's approach was more academic, steeped in history and lore. That made them a good team since one often noticed what the other overlooked.

"Chris and the sheriff both mentioned how bad luck haunts South Fork. Maybe it's more than bad luck," Travis said. "Maybe we need to think whether there's something twisted about the *place*."

"Genius loci? Elemental? There are a lot of land spirits."

"Chris said that the recent attacks have happened closer together timewise, but there's been a long history of bloody deaths around here," Travis mused aloud. "Some of that goes with the dangers of farming and mining, but even the locals think it's too much. Barring a bunch of homegrown serial killers over several generations, it makes me wonder if there isn't a taint to the land itself."

"I guess we'll find out."

Travis parked in front of the feed store, and they got out, flipping up their hoods to keep the worst of the rain at bay. "They said Kendall's attack happened toward the side of the lot—makes sense if he parked his car out of the way for customers."

They separated to cover territory faster, still close enough for backup if needed. Rain and the fire department's cleanup had washed away the blood. Brent knew Travis was opening his psychic abilities to search for ghosts or pick up on images left behind by trauma.

Wish you were here, Danny. You've always been my extra set of eyes. Brent felt a pang of loneliness for his twin's ghost.

No matter how Travis teased him, Brent was hardly a human demon detector, just like despite his mediumistic talent, Travis wasn't a ghost scanner. Demons cost Brent his parents and his brother. They tried to kill him and his team in Iraq and dogged his steps during his time with the FBI and police. He'd finally stopped running, choosing to fight the demons instead.

Both men carried salt, iron, and holy water. Travis had an advantage as a former priest with exorcisms, but Brent knew how to fight with weapons that could weaken demons and force them to flee. He could exorcise a demon as a last resort, but with less certain results than Travis.

Brent glimpsed motion out of the corner of his eye and pivoted to face...nothing.

Travis caught the movement and turned, alert for trouble.

"Thought I saw something," Brent said, searching the brush around the edge of the lot. Nothing moved, and while they remained still for several minutes, he didn't hear anything rustling that might suggest an animal or a bird.

"Don't take any chances," Travis warned, as if Brent needed the reminder.

"I'm not picking up any traces of demons," Travis added. "No sulfur, none of their residual energy."

"Are you reading anything else?"

A queasy look crossed Travis's face. "Unfortunately, yes."

Brent moved protectively close as Travis made his way a little farther down the lot's edge.

Travis stopped and stared at an empty spot on the gravel lot, looking as if he might throw up.

"What?" Brent asked.

"You can't see them?" Travis pointed. Brent shook his head. "Do you remember the demon maggots back in Cooper City?"

"Been trying to forget, thanks. Both of us could see those. Are they here?" Brent looked around quickly, not wanting to meet up with those creatures again.

Travis turned away and closed his eyes as if he were willing his gorge not to rise. "Remember how the witness said that Kendall kept stomping around like something had gone up his pant leg and then seemed to be hacking away at whatever he saw?"

Brent nodded, peering in vain at the spot that held Travis's attention.

"There's a heap of maggots that are the size of a man's head, and they're moving."

"Travis—"

"Ghost maggots. Or whatever you want to call them. They look plenty real to me, and I can sense that they're a manifestation." Travis still sounded sick. "If Kendall saw them without any warning, I can believe they looked and felt real to him."

"That's not normal. Maggots are gross, but they don't usually attack people."

Travis shrugged, looking like he had gotten past the danger of losing his lunch. "If they swarmed, I imagine it would feel like an attack. We don't know what other senses they triggered. Doc Medved said Kendall had circulation problems, so maybe he was afraid of losing a foot or having it go gangrenous."

"Psychic maggots?"

"I don't think they're regular ghosts, and they're not the demonic sort we fought in Cooper City." Travis backed up to a careful distance. "Maybe his fears gave the energy its form."

"Then why are they still in that shape? That's not my fear—or yours," Brent asked.

Travis frowned as he studied the image only he could see. "Curious. Maybe once it's called into its shape, it remains until being dispelled. Or maybe that particular shape is an echo of something from long ago just waiting to be given form."

"What does that?"

"I don't know—yet. But I'm going to find out." Travis sighed. "We'd better get rid of it in case anyone else can see it."

He pulled out a canister of salt from beneath his rain slicker while Brent leveled his shotgun loaded with salt rounds in the general direction.

"If you want me to shoot, point at what I'm supposed to hit since I can't see it," Brent told him.

This time, Travis didn't bother with banishment. He launched right into the exorcism and doused the ghost maggots with a generous spray of salt.

Brent heard something that sounded like a combination of hissing snakes and buzzing cicadas an instant before the writhing mass of undead maggots became visible. He held his fire, fearing that blasting the heap apart might cause worse problems.

"Keep going! I think it's hurting them!" he yelled to Travis.

Travis kept chanting, and the hiss-buzz rose to a deafening level as the heaving ball of larvae expanded and contracted. This time, Brent fired, hoping the salt would weaken the building spectral energy.

The sound of the blast reverberated, and the shell hit the center of the maggot ball, vaporizing those with direct contact and launching a spray of undead slugs into the air to fall in wriggling gobbets as Travis finished the ritual.

"*Audi nos!*"

With the last words of the rite, the manifestation vanished. Travis and Brent couldn't stop themselves from frantically brushing off their clothing and patting down their arms and legs, assuring that none of the creatures remained.

"Holy shit," Brent muttered. "At least we didn't try to chop ourselves up."

"We knew the maggots weren't real. We didn't fully believe in them, so they couldn't hurt us," Travis replied with an expression that suggested he was filing that detail away for further examination.

"We've got company," Brent warned.

"What the hell is going on?" A slender, gray-haired man wearing a feed store employee vest strode toward them. His name tag read "Tom."

Brent turned slightly so that the large lettering on the back proclaiming "Sheriff" was plainly visible.

"Sheriff Calabrese sent us out to take a look at where the death occurred," Travis said smoothly, with a conciliatory smile. "We're investigators from Pittsburgh. A raccoon charged us and looked rabid, so my partner shot at it. Can't be too careful."

Tom stared into the scrub. "Did you scare it off?"

"Yeah," Brent replied. "It won't be back." He crossed his fingers, hoping that was true.

"That's good," Tom allowed, no longer eyeing them with suspicion. "But you gave us a start when we heard the shot. Been too many strange things going on around here."

"Were you working the night Zeke Kendall died?" Travis asked.

The man nodded. "Yeah. Worked with him all evening. Zeke didn't seem any different than he ever was—until he cut himself up. I can't imagine what made him do it." He shivered, and Brent didn't think the revulsion was faked.

"Are you from South Fork?" Travis asked and got a nod in reply. "What happened to Zeke—does it remind you of anything that might have happened in the past?"

Tom raised an eyebrow. "You're asking about One-leg John, ain't you?"

Travis shrugged. "Tell us, please."

The feed store man glanced back toward the building, but no one seemed to care he'd walked off the job. He swiped a hand across his mouth in a nervous gesture. "I don't think the younger folk have heard the story, but my grandpa used to tell us when we sat around the campfire. Wanted to scare the bejeezus out of us, most likely."

He cleared his throat. "After the war, ol' John came home not quite right in the head, if you take my meaning. Shell shock, or whatever they call it these days. Took a lot of shrapnel to his legs, but they managed to patch him up. Or so they thought."

Tom gave them a crafty look. "One night, John was fidgety. Couldn't seem to keep his mind on anything, jumpy as a cat on a hot tin roof. One of the guys working with him said there was a real bad smell coming off him, and it got worse as the night went on. Then round about closing time, John lost it. He started jumping up and down and screaming, and he grabbed a hunting knife when he ran out of the building."

Brent could tell Tom was working up to the big finale. He wondered whether the story had faded from popular knowledge before Calabrese's time.

"Of course, everyone followed him, wondering what's going on.

He was still dancing around and shouting, and then he started slicing up his bad leg with that knife. A couple of the guys ran up to try to stop him, but the smell was even worse." Tom looked like he was enjoying his salacious tale.

"When he cut into his leg, it had gone rotten. That's why it stank so bad. They said that pus and maggots poured out. John kept slicing, cut into the bone, and finally got an artery. Bled out right on the spot. Folks said that when they opened him up at the hospital, he was full of worms." Tom stood back, awaiting their reaction.

"When was this?" Brent asked.

"Maybe 1946, not long after the boys came home from overseas," Tom replied. "Before my time. Like I said—younger folk might not know the story, but it sure made an impression on my grandad."

"Thank you," Travis said. "That helps a lot."

Tom raised an eyebrow. "Really? Well, there's no telling what suits folks. Just don't be shooting off guns in the lot."

"I think we're done," Travis assured him. Tom gave him a nod and headed back to the store. Brent salted the area around where the ghost maggots had turned up, just in case, although the steady rain would sluice away the granules soon enough.

They shook the water off as best they could before getting back into the Crown Vic.

"What did you make of all that?" Brent asked as Travis pulled out of the lot and headed for the next site.

"I think there's a connection between One-leg John and what happened to Kendall. It's too much of a coincidence," Travis replied.

"If Tom's memory is correct, John died almost seventy years ago," Brent pointed out. "Why wait until now for a re-run?"

"Maybe Kendall wasn't the only one to die like this. Given what seems to pass for 'normal' here, maybe the other occurrences got lost among all the general crazy." Travis stopped at the town's single traffic light and waited for a few cars to go through the intersection.

"You think we're going to find something similar with Becca and

Rick? Or other events in town history?" Brent suspected as much, but he wanted confirmation.

"Maybe. We need to test the hypothesis. I'm curious to see what the librarian can find when we finish," Travis said.

Brent expected the diner to be busy, given that it was mid-afternoon, but the rain seemed to have kept most people at home. They found a parking space to one side of the lot and walked over to the spot the sheriff had reported finding the body.

"We might drown by the time we're through," Brent grumbled as cold rain trickled under his collar despite the coat.

"Doubt we'd be that lucky," Travis replied, looking cold and miserable.

They walked around the area where Becca had died. "I don't know what we're looking for," Brent admitted.

"Guess we'll know it when we see it."

Fifteen minutes of fruitless searching later, Brent swore under his breath. The damp cold made him shiver and darkened his mood. He concentrated, trying to sense dark energies, but did not feel the dangerous shadows he had at the feed store or near the road.

Travis's outcry brought Brent running. "What's the matter? What do you see?" Brent prodded, gripping Travis by the shoulders as his partner sank to his haunches. Tremors ran through Travis's form, and his unfocused gaze stared into the distance.

"Knives," Travis mumbled. "Sharp. So much blood. He keeps on stabbing..."

Brent knew from experience that he could do little when Travis was gripped by a vision except to protect him and wait it out. Neither salt nor exorcism would make a difference since the vision wasn't imposed by an outside spirit and couldn't be banished. This was Travis's mind and part of his psychic gift, an ability to catch snippets in time and witness things past, present, or future that he would otherwise have no way to know.

Travis's gaze tracked something only he could see. "Thank you," he murmured before he slumped forward.

When Travis relaxed, Brent knew the vision had passed. "Come on." He helped Travis stand. "Let's get some hot coffee—and pie. The investigation can wait long enough for you to get your feet under you again."

"I'm fine," Travis protested, although his pallor and wide eyes betrayed the lie.

"Well, I'm hungry and cold—and I want to go inside." Brent knew Travis would turn down taking a break on his account but wouldn't force Brent to be uncomfortable.

Travis gave in and followed Brent inside. The diner had a soda fountain vibe, with Formica-topped chrome-trimmed tables, red swivel seats at the counter, and a tile floor. Brent nudged Travis toward the counter, focused more on getting him to consume sugar and caffeine than nabbing a private place to talk.

Once they ordered—coffee for both, cherry pie for Travis, and apple for Brent—he bumped elbows with his friend. "Better?"

Travis grunted. "Pie helps. Thanks."

Since Travis polished off dessert in record time and downed a couple of cups of java, Brent felt reassured that the shock of the vision hadn't caused lasting damage. They paid the bill and retreated to the Crown Vic, where Brent held out his hand for the keys.

"I'm fine," Travis protested.

"I'm sure you are," Brent lied. "But it's okay to give yourself some time to bounce back. We don't have far to go—just over to Rick's trailer. Take a minute and rest. We'll need your mojo at full strength if anything happens."

Travis gave in with a glare that wasn't quite as menacing as he might have intended. Brent could tell Travis hadn't pulled himself together yet and stayed silent during the drive so Travis could rest or meditate.

"A woman was stabbed in that parking lot," Travis said finally. "Multiple times—the attack was savage. Personal. I saw her ghost, and she linked me to the memory like a record on repeat. The killer knew her—ex-boyfriend or husband. He was furious. She didn't stand a chance," he added, choking up.

"There were other women killed in that lot over the years—it makes sense, doesn't it? All-night diner, waitress comes off the evening shift, no one's around. Perfect place for an ambush. I'm betting that they all knew their killers. I think what I saw is important, and I believe it's a clue."

"But Becca wasn't killed by an old flame," Brent countered. "The witnesses said no one was around."

"Maybe enough evil stained the energy there that, with the right circumstances, it took on a life of its own," Travis replied.

Brent nodded. "Well, that's terrifying. How the hell do we fight that?"

Travis shook his head. "We don't know everything yet. Maybe we'll find something at the next stop that helps us pull everything together."

Calabrese had entrusted them with the key to Rick's trailer since the official crime scene had been released. Brent couldn't shake a sense of foreboding as they drove back the lane. He had learned to take his gut feelings seriously—doing so had saved his life more times than he could count.

"Guess he liked his privacy," Travis observed as they parked in the driveway, turning around so they could leave fast if the need arose.

"Pretty spot," Brent replied, taking in the woods that surrounded the trailer. "Maybe Rick just liked nature."

"Grab the shotgun and iron. I can't see what's here, but I can damn well feel it," Travis said, reaching for salt, holy water, and a piece of rebar.

Crime scene tape fluttered in the wind. Brent could enjoy solitude as much as anyone, but the area around the trailer felt unnaturally silent as if everything around them was holding its breath.

"Let's save going inside for last," Travis said. "Don't want to get trapped in there."

Brent nodded, glad they were thinking the same thing. "He got badly hurt out here—that's where the bad juju should be."

Brent made a mental note to ask Travis why the spirits of the recent murder victims hadn't stuck around, but the entities that killed them persisted. *Something is definitely fucked up around here, and if we don't figure it out, there'll be more bodies to bury.*

Travis and Brent moved warily, doing a sweep of the small grassy area in front of Rick's old travel trailer. The rain hadn't let up; still a steady drizzle. A security light on a telephone pole glowed thanks to the solid cloud cover.

The trailer looked well-maintained despite its age. So did the worn pickup truck parked nearby, a vehicle Rick might never be able to drive again. Bushes and plants along the front of the trailer suggested permanence. In the back, Brent saw the remnants of a small vegetable garden. Whatever had brought Rick out here to the woods, he seemed to have found stability and made a home, and it angered Brent that the attack had stolen those away.

"Got colder," Travis warned, and Brent realized he could see his breath. Frost spread across the wet grass, and just near the trailer, the rain turned to sleet.

Brent caught a glimpse of a gray figure taking shape. He raised his shotgun and fired, figuring that each volley weakened the ghost.

Travis laid down a circle of rope that had been soaked in salt and colloidal silver, the only way they could protect themselves on wet ground. The warded area was large enough for both of them, and Brent stepped inside, in no hurry to be thrown around again.

"Next time, let the ghost form," Travis told him. "Let's get a look at Hammer Guy."

"As long as he keeps his distance," Brent muttered. "We don't know how strong he is."

Travis closed his eyes, and Brent knew his partner wasn't waiting for the ghost to make an appearance—he was calling to the spirit, inviting it to show itself.

"We've got company," Brent said quietly.

The ghost appeared about six feet away and gradually grew more solid. The grizzled old man matched Tim's description, looking like what Brent had seen on TV as a "miner forty-niner," complete with suspenders, wide-brimmed hat, and a wild beard. The spirit's eyes held malice, and there was no missing the sledgehammer he held in one hand.

"We can send you to your rest," Travis told the spirit. "You can move on."

The specter's form shuddered, and suddenly he stood just outside the salt circle.

"Watch out!" Brent shouted, trading a blast of the shotgun for the ghost's swing of his deadly hammer as he pulled Travis into a crouch. He felt the swish of air as the hammer sailed over their heads, and the apparition vanished.

"How the hell—" he started, wondering how the revenant managed to swing his hammer into what should have been warded space.

"Not the usual ghost—maybe not a ghost at all. I don't think it's a demon, either. Some kind of spirit creature?" Travis replied in a grim tone. "He'll be back."

"Plan B?" Brent asked.

Travis gave a curt nod.

Brent kept the shotgun close at hand, but they knew now that this spirit was too strong to be dispelled by mere salt. He pulled out a hand-held flamethrower from the gear bag and stood ready as Travis launched into the exorcism. Fire worked on many supernatural creatures, and whatever this was, it manifested solidly enough to harm the living.

The miner's spirit creature wasn't a demon. But a second before the apparition appeared again, Brent swore he heard Danny scream a warning in his mind.

Travis's cadence never faltered, even as Brent loosed a torrent of flame at the spirit and trapped it within the fire. "Hurry! This thing has a small tank." He mentally counted the seconds the gas canister would last.

Travis didn't react, but he picked up the pace of the ritual as the miner's spirit writhed, engulfed by flames.

"It's working," Brent said as the edges of the ghost began to burn like charred paper.

Brent knew the ritual by heart. Travis was nearly done, and the creature had started to fade. *Only a few more lines.*

The flamethrower died.

Brent ducked as the hammer swung once more. He pushed Travis out of the way, turning so that the impact hit his gear bag instead of his shoulder. The force of the blow still drove him to his knees, and he knew he would be bruised. *Better than a broken arm.*

He dropped the flamethrower and raised the shotgun as Travis shouted the last line of the exorcism in triumph.

The miner screamed in fury as his form dissipated and faded into nothing on the wind.

Brent straightened, feeling sore muscles where the sledgehammer had hit his bag. "Is he gone?"

Travis rose from where Brent had knocked him to his knees. "Yes. As far as I can tell." He frowned. "You're hurt."

"I've had worse." Brent stretched and grimaced at the discomfort.

"You've been better too. Thank you. I know you protected me."

"If I let the ghost take out the exorcist, we're all up shit creek." Brent managed a smile.

"Are you okay to walk?"

"Yeah, but I'd rather not run for a while," Brent admitted.

"Let's head for the library. We can dry out and get warm, and maybe if Calabrese's wife is working she can help us track down some history. I've got ibuprofen in the car."

Brent knew he was moving like an old man, and his back hurt like hell. He also knew that if he hadn't deflected the blow, it would have been far worse, but that was cold comfort at the moment.

He swallowed the pills as soon as Travis dug out the bottle from the glove compartment and then got settled into the passenger seat.

"Want to bet there's a mine nearby that had a fatal accident?" Travis asked.

Brent could tell his partner was surreptitiously checking him over, making sure his injuries weren't worse than he had let on.

"Sounds like a working theory to me." Brent sighed as he resigned himself to nothing being comfortable.

"We'll make sure we get ice before we go to Chris's house so maybe you'll be able to move in the morning," Travis promised.

"That sounds really good," Brent replied, biting back a groan when he tried to find a more comfortable way to sit.

"Talk to me," Travis said. "There's something you're not saying."

Brent sighed. "There at the end, when the flamethrower died, I could have sworn I heard Danny yell a warning in my mind. That's how I knew to duck."

"Maybe being worried about you was what he needed to push through from wherever he's been," Travis mused. "I don't doubt that he'll come back to you if he's able."

"I hope so. I miss him."

Travis pulled into the library lot and grimaced to find the only open spots far from the door. "Looks like we found the hot hangout in town—besides Fisher's."

"Makes sense," Brent said. "Most of the people here are older. The library probably has community programs. Maybe it's social hour for people who don't day drink."

Brent did his best not to move stiffly, suspecting he failed badly. He knew he hadn't broken anything, but they couldn't afford for him to be off his game, not when they still didn't understand the threat they were up against.

South Fork Library's entrance hallway was lined with bulletin boards featuring upcoming programs and reminding patrons that they could also borrow ebooks, audiobooks, and DVDs. Two glass cases featured artwork from children and adults, proudly emblazoned with the names of the artists.

Travis paused to read some of the notices. "For a small town, there's a lot going on. The librarians are doing their best to offer reasons to stay positive."

"From what Chris said, this town needs all the help it can get with that," Brent replied.

The inside was painted in cheerful colors. Toward the back in the children's section, murals of animals, sailing ships, rockets, and castles covered the walls. Over to one side, three computer terminals were busy with patrons. Rows of bookshelves suggested that despite limited resources, the library had managed to acquire a good-sized collection.

Brent saw more people here than anywhere else in South Fork. Mothers with small children in the back, retirees reading in the comfortable armchairs scattered around the open spaces, people standing in line to check out books.

"Kudos to the librarians. They've done a helluva good job with what they've got to work with," Travis said.

Brent knew his partner's inner academic appreciated libraries and bookstores. "They've put a lot of effort into making this a bright spot," Brent replied. *Lord knows, South Fork needs that.*

They got the worst of the water off their jackets before heading for the main desk.

"We're looking for Tammy Calabrese," Brent said to the middle-aged librarian who waited on them after they worked their way through the line.

She gave them a look Brent realized as sizing up the strangers for threat. "Stay here. I'll see if she's available."

Brent figured their chances were fifty-fifty of Tammy coming out to see them, but he relaxed when a woman close to their age bustled out of the back room. Her dark hair was caught back in a clip, and she wore a t-shirt that read "Free your mind—read a banned book."

"You must be the guys from out of town Tony said might stop in." She greeted them with a smile. "I'm Tammy."

They introduced themselves, and Tammy motioned for them to

follow her to a small conference room. "What can I do for you, gentlemen?"

Brent and Travis carefully hung their wet coats over the backs of chairs where the dampness wouldn't harm anything and pulled up seats across the table from Tammy.

"We're trying to find news articles or obituaries that might help us track unusual deaths," Brent said.

Tammy gave a bitter chuckle. "South Fork is the epicenter of 'unusual deaths.' Can you narrow it down?"

Brent filed that comment away for later. "We're looking into the attack on Rick and the other two recent deaths. Is there a way to find out if someone else died in those locations long ago?"

Tammy looked at them with narrowed eyes, thinking. "Probably —but it'll take some digging. Tony told me the two of you have 'unique' skills. You think it's some kind of malicious spirit?"

Brent felt relieved that she hadn't dismissed them out of hand. "We're not sure yet, but that's one theory."

"In its heyday, South Fork had coal mines, a rock quarry, a busy railroad depot for cargo and passengers, and a lumber mill. All of those are dangerous. But in my opinion, the usual dangers don't explain the number of deaths and accidents that happen here in an average year," Tammy told them. Brent wondered if she felt relieved to have someone who would believe her speculation.

"This town has had more than its share of bad luck, going back as far as we've got records. Mine disasters. Railroad wrecks. Explosions or bridge collapses or fires. Outbreaks of one type or another. Multi-car pile-ups. I've been trying to trace the phenomena back through the years for a while now. Tony knew that when he sent you here— me and my gruesome little research project," Tammy added with a grim chuckle.

"We'd love to see your research." Brent felt like they might have just turned a corner. "Have you come to any conclusions?"

"From what I can piece together, this place has had a higher mortality rate per capita than other towns in this area, especially ones with similar industries. It's not my imagination. It goes way back. We've had fires and floods and drought. Why did people stay? The jobs paid reasonably well—until they vanished—and a lot of folks didn't have anywhere else to go," Tammy said.

"Is there a starting point? Did something *make* South Fork unlucky?" Travis asked.

"There's a story—might or might not be true—that the Native Americans who lived around here tried to talk the first settlers out of building the town where it is. Of course, they didn't listen." Tammy sighed. "Sounds like the beginning of every Stephen King novel, doesn't it? At least I can tell you that as far as anyone has ever found out, there is no ancient burying ground under the city. Miles of mine tunnels—yes."

"Did the bad luck get worse at a certain point?" Brent picked up the line of questioning.

Tammy nodded. "In the last five years, there's a definite uptick."

"Do you have a theory about why?"

She paused, tapping her finger against the table as if deciding what to say. "I can't prove it, but I think it's got something to do with the hospital."

"Why?" They'd run across plenty of haunted hospitals or abandoned sanitariums, but so far, the South Fork facility hadn't come up much in conversation.

"All the accidents, suicides, and unexplained injuries go through the hospital," Tammy said. "I'd think something like that would leave a stain—and ghosts. The hospital's mortality rates are off the charts—just one of the reasons it's finally closing."

Brent leaned forward. "Where would the hospital's old autopsy records be stored? I mean really old—like more than forty years ago."

Tammy thought for a moment. "We've got the town newspaper on microfiche going back more than a hundred years—you can find obituaries in those, but people often leave out the cause of death if it's bloody. The autopsy records themselves? Either Doc Medved has them squirreled away somewhere, or they're wherever the hospital has its long-term storage. I can try to find out."

"Thank you," Brent said as a dark possibility occurred to him. "Do you know if the hospital here in town ever offered any special government programs for veterans that weren't commonly provided elsewhere?"

Tammy looked puzzled. "Like clinical trials? I'm not sure. I'll add it to my list."

"I'd appreciate it." Brent caught the sidelong look Travis sent him and knew his partner guessed the thoughts behind his question.

"How can we help? We didn't come here to dump a bunch of research on you," Travis added.

Tammy tapped her pencil against her lips for a minute, deep in thought. "There might be an easier way to come at this. You're not interested in all deaths—just the weird ones. Those are likely to have required a call to the sheriff's office. If you find the names of the victims and the dates of the deaths, it would make it a lot quicker to cross-check autopsy records and news coverage."

Travis grinned. "You're a genius. Think you can persuade the sheriff to give us access?"

"I just might have an in," Tammy said with a wink. "They're public access, but not always quick to find, so I'll give the office a call and get someone to find them for you." She pulled a sheet of paper from a notepad and scribbled down a phone number.

"You also need to talk to Liz Bowers. She's been a nurse at St. Benedict's Hospital for twenty years, and she's seen a lot of the weirdest stuff. She's my bowling buddy, and she runs the Tuesday night bunco game. We go way back. I'll give her a heads-up that you're looking for information, and have her meet you at Fisher's when her shift's over. She'll know where to look for the stuff people want to hide."

Tammy slid the sheet over to Brent, who pocketed it and wrote their numbers on another paper for her.

"I'll text you when I've got news," she told them. "Why don't you head over to the sheriff's office? I'll let Tony know you're on your way."

The rain hadn't let up when they headed back to their car, and the parking lot seemed even more full than before. "The library here is a happening place," Brent observed.

"That's a good thing. They've obviously tried hard to make it a sanctuary and be welcoming. But then again, I'm always a pushover for libraries," Travis admitted.

"Even secret occult ones?" Brent teased, knowing that Travis had access to the hidden Vatican library in Pittsburgh.

Travis made a face as if he'd sucked on a lemon. "In that case, it's the books—definitely not the company they keep." Travis disliked the Sinistram nearly as much as Brent loathed CHARON.

"I had a thought about how to shave some time off the records search," Brent said as they drove the short distance to the sheriff's office. "If we search on the deed history for the three locations we know about, then we'd at least have three data points to look for bizarre deaths at those sites. There are probably a lot more, but that might confirm our theory and give us something to work with."

"I like that. How about I do the deed search while you start in on the police records. I hope they have coffee. No matter how we approach it, we're going to be slogging through a lot of files," Travis replied.

Brent had given up all hope of getting completely dry as they hurried into the sheriff's office. To their surprise, Calabrese was not only expecting them; he looked ready to leave.

"Good. You're here. Tammy called me. I think you've got a good idea, but it'll have to wait," Calabrese said. "You can come with me— we need to go. We've got another weird one." Brent thought the sheriff looked tired and worn.

"To the hospital?" Brent feared he already knew the answer.

Tony shook his head. "Not this time. But we've got witnesses. C'mon. You'll get a first-hand look. It's—bad. Good thing you've got a strong stomach."

CHAPTER FIVE

AMBULANCE LIGHTS REFLECTED in the windows of the split-level house. The neighborhood looked like it would have been quiet any other evening, but few people would be getting a good night's sleep tonight.

"Sorry about the circumstances," Calabrese said when a blonde woman in her forties met them on the sidewalk. "Give us a few minutes with the ambulance crew, and we'll be inside to talk with you." She nodded and went back into the house next door.

"Must be nice to work in a big city where you don't know the people you pull out of a car wreck or arrest on a domestic call," Calabrese said with a sigh. "Unfortunately, every single fucking call-out is someone I know—someone I grew up with. It sucks."

Travis and Brent followed the sheriff to the ambulance. The crew's lack of urgency gave Travis the answer to the victim's condition.

Even with the rain, blood soaked the patio. A crimson-stained claw hammer lay on the pavers next to the body of a woman whose throat looked as if it had been torn out by wild animals.

"Talk to me, Cliff. What happened here?" Calabrese said to the older of the two EMTs, a balding man in his early forties.

"I can give you the *what* but not the *why*," Cliff replied, and although he retained his professional composure, Travis could see the man was badly shaken.

"Shelly's left hand is pulverized from being hit with that hammer," Cliff said. "Looks like it was used to tear out her throat too."

"Did anyone get a look at who attacked her?" Calabrese asked.

Travis had the awful feeling he already knew the answer.

"Witnesses say she did it herself." Cliff glanced toward his partner, who silently nodded.

"Holy fuck," Calabrese muttered.

"She was dead when we arrived," Cliff said. "Liz called us—she and some friends saw everything out the window."

A second SUV emblazoned with the sheriff's insignia pulled up and killed the siren and lights. The red-headed man who got out— whom Travis assumed was Calabrese's deputy—looked shell-shocked.

"Jesus," he swore as he joined them. "If this keeps up, there's not going to be anyone left."

"Let's take the photos, go through the drill," Calabrese ordered. "I don't think we're likely to find any evidence besides the hammer, but we need to look."

He made short introductions for Travis and Brent to Bobby, his deputy. "How about you two hold the floodlights and make it easier for us to get the formalities taken care of so Cliff can take the body away."

Travis and Brent spent the next hour cold and wet, hoping none of the lighting equipment had faulty wiring so they didn't end up electrocuted on the wet lawn. Despite the rain and the growing darkness, Calabrese and his deputy gave Shelley the dignity her death deserved, doing their investigation by the book.

When Calabrese finally stood, he couldn't hide how shaken he was. Bobby put the lights away, and Calabrese walked over to Travis and Brent, looking equally bedraggled and miserable.

"Shelly and I went to kindergarten together. Hell, we were in every grade all the way up—South Fork only has one school. Shelly left for a while, got a job in Harrisburg, married a guy there. Then they got a divorce, she lost her job, and ended up here, working data entry at the hospital."

Calabrese shook his head. "I always thought Shelly would be one of the ones who got out. But she got dragged back, like the rest of us."

The ambulance pulled out, carrying Shelly's corpse to the morgue. Bobby followed to handle the paperwork. Calabrese turned and led them toward the house next door to the people who had presumably seen what happened.

"You okay?" Travis asked Brent in a tone just above a whisper. He didn't mention that he could see his partner shivering or that Brent's lips were nearly blue with cold.

"Yeah. Got colder in Iraq than this at night, but at least we didn't have the fucking rain." Brent looked chilled and miserable.

The door opened before Calabrese even had a chance to knock. "Come in, leave your wet coats and shoes by the door." A woman Travis assumed was Tammy's friend Liz ordered. She had short brown hair and bright blue eyes that seemed much older than her mid-thirties. "I've got towels for you to dry off, and we turned up the heat. You've got a choice of coffee or hot chocolate, and no one here will breathe a word if you want a little Irish with that."

They all opted for coffee, but Travis picked up a whiff of whiskey that suggested that Liz and her friends had already spiked their drinks. If they'd actually seen Shelly's death, he didn't begrudge them.

Travis guessed Liz's friends looked to be near her own age, one with shoulder-length blonde hair, and the other with a long, dark braid.

"This is Angie," Liz said with a nod toward the blonde, introducing her friends for Travis and Brent's sakes. "And this is Jamie. It's our weekly bunco night—that's a dice game that's mostly an excuse to drink wine. Tuesdays are our bowling night—our team, the Sure Shots—has been together since we were in high school. Shel was on our team," she added, fighting back tears. Jamie put a hand on Liz's shoulder, and Angie took her hand.

"I'm sorry to have to ask," Calabrese said, and Travis couldn't imagine how painful this was for the sheriff, given everyone's long shared history. "But apparently, you're the only witnesses. Chris asked Travis and Brent to come in from Pittsburgh to lend a hand, given all the strange goings-on. They're specialists."

Liz locked eyes with Travis. "Well, I damn sure hope you're an exorcist, because what's going on in South Fork is straight out of hell."

Travis cleared his throat, not wanting to confirm or deny.

"What happened?" Calabrese prodded gently.

Liz shared a look with her girlfriends and then straightened her shoulders and lifted her head. Travis guessed this was her "nurse" persona, the stoic front she presented amid the heartbreak of hospital work.

"We were playing bunco and dishing the news—splitting a bottle of wine and some munchies," Liz said. "Talked about what happened to Becca and Rick. Jamie said gun sales are up at the hardware store— everyone's on edge. Then we heard screaming."

She paused. "Jamie had a gun in her purse—she's got a permit— and I had a shotgun in the closet. We went out onto the porch, and we saw Shelly on her patio and—oh, God—she had a hammer, and she was smashing her left hand."

Liz bit her lip, steadying herself. "I don't mean like someone does when they mean to drive a nail and miss. She was smacking that hammer down with her full strength, over and over, screaming all the while, but she didn't stop. We yelled to her, but it was like she couldn't hear us or was too lost in her head to know we were there. We should have run over right away, not just stood on the porch. But we couldn't believe it. Didn't seem real. We were frozen."

She closed her eyes. "She screamed louder, and that got us going.

We started over, thinking we could maybe tackle her and get the hammer away, but we were halfway there, and she hit herself in the throat with the claw end." A shudder ran through her body. "No—not just 'hit.' Shelly sank the claw into her neck and *pulled*. Like she meant to rip her throat out—and she did. We didn't touch anything. We ran back here and called 911."

Liz opened her eyes and looked at Calabrese, her gaze begging for answers. "Why? I went out to lunch with her two days ago, and she seemed fine. No new heartbreak, no job problems—situation normal. But fuck, Tony, who kills themself like that? There are a lot easier ways to go."

Liz looked down at her hands clasped so tightly on her lap that the whites of her knuckles showed. Angie and Jamie moved closer, wrapping their arms around her, holding space for her to regain her composure.

After a few moments, Calabrese cleared his throat. "Did any of the rest of you see anything different?"

Angie and Jamie shook their heads. "No," Angie replied. "Just like Liz said."

"She kept on hitting," Jamie murmured, clearly upset. "One hit like that would make most people throw up or pass out—maybe both. She had to have broken bones on each strike. She kept on going until her hand...there was just pulp. I don't understand."

Travis hung back, feeling very much the outsider. A glance at Brent confirmed his partner felt the same. He let Calabrese lead the investigation and watched for anything that might bear further examination.

"One more question, and I'll leave you alone tonight—although I'll need to get your official statements tomorrow down at the station. Do you know anything about the history of the house Shelly lived in?" Calabrese asked.

The women looked up, seemingly surprised at his change in direction. "Shelly bought it from Mrs. Peterson," Liz said, squinting as she concentrated. "Mrs. Peterson had lived there since I was in middle school—only sold because she had to go into a nursing home."

"There was a man before her—a widower," Jamie supplied. "I remember because my mom brought him chicken soup once when he was really sick during the winter."

"Jacob Straub," Angie added. "Yes. I only remember because he gave out good Halloween candy even though I imagine his own kids were all grown up by the time we came along."

"I think Mr. Straub might have bought it from the original owners," Liz said. "And now that I think about it, I wonder if there wasn't something shady about them—just reinterpreting things my mom said from an adult's perspective. She wasn't going to let us Trick-or-Treat at his house because of something the previous owner did until we proved a new person lived there. As far as I ever heard, Mr. Straub and Mrs. Peterson were good people."

Travis saw Brent making a note on his phone to check the house's deed. "Thank you," Travis said, sure that Liz and her friends needed time alone to grieve. "If you think of anything else that seemed... strange in a spooky kind of way...please let the sheriff know, and he'll pass it along to us."

Liz gave him an appraising look as if trying to figure out where Travis was coming from and too overwhelmed to do more than silently question.

By the time they walked back to the sheriff's Jeep, the ambulance was gone. Calabrese crossed the crime scene tape to meet them. "I'm going to be here for a while. I called Tammy, and she's going to swing by to pick you up and take you to Fisher's. If I find out more, I'll meet you there or at Chris's house later."

The sheriff ran a hand through his hair. "It's been a helluva week so far...and I don't think it's likely to get better."

A blue F150 pickup stopped at the curb, and Travis saw Tammy waving at them to get in. They climbed inside, apologizing for getting the seat wet.

"You oughta see what happens during deer hunting season," Tammy laughed off their apology. "It wipes off."

Tammy's smile faded as she looked toward the rain-soaked patio and the crime scene tape. "Sometimes I think it won't end until there's no one left in town," she said to no one in particular. "I'd sure like to know what someone did to get the town so cursed."

Travis understood the grief beneath the anger and marveled again at the stubbornness—or desperation—of the people who refused to give up their home to the darkness that stalked South Fork.

"We're hoping we can figure that out—and make it stop." Travis frowned. "I saw two churches in town. Can I ask—"

"Pastor Horton at the Methodist church is a nice man but shallow as a puddle," Tammy replied, navigating the rain-slick streets. "He can mouth the words at weddings, funerals, and baptisms, but don't expect *perspective*. When a tornado hit the trailer park outside of town a few years back, and everyone in town knew someone who either died or lost everything, Pastor Horton decided to start a series of sermons on the church's *stained glass windows*. Because that's what we all needed to hear at a time like that." Her voice dripped sarcasm.

Travis winced at the well-earned condemnation. Although he had shed the collar years ago, he had no patience for clergy who ignored the needs of their flock.

"And the Catholic church?" Travis hated to ask, yet needed to know.

Tammy sighed. "I think this town broke Father Prochazka. My family wasn't devout, but I remember people spoke well of him when I was a kid. Then...to tell you the honest truth, I think South Fork cost him his faith. I mean, why should he be the only one left in town who believes?"

She shook her head. "He just kinda *dimmed* over time, like the light inside went out. Started looking for Jesus in the bottom of a bottle. Can't say I blame him—he's not the first person in town to do that, won't be the last."

Tammy tapped the steering wheel. "People don't really expect any miracles; they're just trying to hold things together for them and theirs, one day at a time. Doesn't seem a lot to ask, now does it?"

"Why do people stay?" Brent asked from the back seat, his tone making it clear that his question was sincere.

"Because it's home. Yeah, there are some folks who are too old to start over or don't have anywhere else to go. Every year there are fewer kids born, fewer to graduate. Most of them light out of town like their tails are on fire—and I can't blame them," Tammy said.

"Some have family here to care for and can't afford to move. I guess the rest of us are just too stubborn for our own good," she said with a bitter laugh. "You ever heard of Centralia—the abandoned town with the hundred-year mine fire burning underground? I imagine South Fork'll be a ghost town eventually, but it won't be a coal fire that drives us out. There's something infernal in the bones of this place, and it's getting stronger."

She pulled up to Fisher's, which had a dozen cars parked in front, all older models. "Come by the library in the morning. I'll be thinking about what materials to pull for you tonight. I like mysteries—and I haven't had a good challenge in a long while."

Travis and Brent got out, and Tammy rolled down the window on the passenger side, leaning across the bench seat. "You two be careful, you hear?"

They nodded, and she drove off, leaving them to navigate the muddy gravel on their way inside.

This time, Travis and Brent took seats at the bar, more interested for the moment in hearing what others were saying than debriefing. Chris acknowledged them with a nod and brought them hot coffee that smelled of whiskey.

"To take the chill off," he said.

Travis closed his eyes as he took a sip and tuned in to the conversations around him.

"...couldn't believe it when Liz called me and told me the news."

"...Shelly and I were in band together. Can't believe she's gone."

"...this town is like a bad horror movie, only it never ends."

"...Shel and I went to prom junior year—remember? Whatever happened, she deserved better."

Travis caught snatches of other discussions—about the weather, sports scores, or the headlines. Quiet voices mentioned the recent trio of deaths in a near-whisper as if not wanting to provoke bad luck. It didn't require a psychic to pick up the tension, a combination of fear, worry, and desperation.

He knew the two of them had drawn attention—outsiders were easy to spot. Travis suspected that only their borrowed sheriff's department rain slickers kept the questions at bay, for which he was thankful.

"Specialty of the house." Chris set down two steaming plates of pierogi, *haluski*, and kielbasa in front of them. "The pierogis are house-made, garlic-potato filling. We always sell out."

Travis and Brent thanked him, and Travis enjoyed the simple comfort of the hot, filled dumplings, buttered cabbage with onions, and savory meat. From the way Brent dug into his meal, Travis guessed his partner felt the same way.

They were nearly finished with the meal when the door opened, and a gust of cold wind swept inside. A man in a black slicker with a broad-brimmed bucket hat and Wellington boots stomped in and shook off like a wet dog. He let the hat fall back on its strap and unbuttoned the coat, revealing a dark shirt and a clerical collar.

A few of the patrons murmured a greeting as he passed, others nodded, and some didn't look up from their drinks. He responded with a half-hearted wave and walked up to the end of the bar, not far from where Travis and Brent sat. If the priest noticed them, he didn't show it.

Guess that's Father Prochazka, Travis thought. The clergyman looked to be in his mid-sixties, bald with a fringe of short gray hair, clean-shaven. Old sorrow swam in the man's light blue eyes, and he carried himself as if the weight of the world rested on his narrow shoulders.

"You get it?" he asked Horvath, who nodded and pulled a paper bag from beneath the bar. He set it on the counter, and the man laid down a few bills, clearly familiar with the cost. "Keep the change. Thanks."

The bag clinked when Father Prochazka picked it up, suggesting more than one fifth of liquor inside. The older man's expression set in defiance as if daring anyone to comment. No one seemed to care. He made his way back to the door and disappeared into the storm.

"You think there's a place in hell for being your priest's dealer?" Chris asked as he refilled their coffee and cleared away their plates.

"Kinda doubt that's high on the list of sins," Brent said. "Whatever gets him through the night. Not gonna judge."

They took their coffee to a table in the back, and Travis dodged out to the Crown Vic long enough to come back with their laptops. Since they were staying with Chris, there was nowhere to go until the bar closed.

Customers came and went. Some stayed for an hour or two, while others stopped to chat and left with takeout bags. Travis wondered if the diner was equally busy or if some of the patrons who bellied up to the bar had eaten dinner and came to Fisher's for a nightcap.

While Travis searched deeds, Brent looked for historical documents. The surprisingly strong Wi-Fi signal made the effort less arduous than usual since they often struggled with glitchy internet and poor reception while on the road.

Travis began with the deed to Rick Donaldson's lot, tracing it back through foreclosures and title disputes until he hit paydirt in the 1920s and let out a low whistle.

"What?" Brent glanced up from his screen.

"The trailer's lot was on top of a defunct coal mine," Travis said.

"Most of Pennsylvania is on top of a defunct coal mine," Brent snarked.

"True. But this one had an especially abysmal record for cave-ins, bad air, and accidents. And back in 1933, a guy named Gustav Schmidt went psycho with a sledgehammer on his fellow miners.

Bludgeoned six men to death, gravely injured another four, before Gustav threw himself into an open shaft and died." Travis cleared his throat. "*Presumably* died—they never recovered the body."

"Yeah, what could go wrong?" Brent muttered. "You think Gustav's ghost came back to take a whack at Rick?"

Lizzie Borden took an axe and gave her father forty whacks...

Travis turned his laptop around to show Brent his screen. "This is a photo of the mining company's employees a few months before the incident. Gustav is the guy on the far right, second row."

Brent leaned forward for a closer look, and his eyes widened. "Looks exactly like the guy we got rid of."

Travis nodded. "Yeah. And get this—Donaldson picked up the land from an auction on the cheap because the previous owner 'fell down a sinkhole into a previously-sealed mine shaft' and disappeared."

Pennsylvania was undermined with thousands of miles of forgotten mining tunnels from hundreds of long-gone companies whose records were lost in fires, floods, or simply discarded.

Sinkholes were common enough that many mortgage companies required mine subsidence insurance in case the living room suddenly vanished into a bottomless pit. The mines themselves were the tombs of miners killed in falls, accidents, cave-ins, explosions, and suffocation from toxic gases.

They're like the poor man's version of the Roman Catacombs.

"I've been trying to find out anything I can about the history of St. Benedict's Hospital," Brent said as Travis took back his laptop. "Since I can't get to the police records until tomorrow." He shook his head. "I had forgotten how small towns work when everyone knows everyone else."

"It's got its good points—and its bad ones," Travis agreed. "But it certainly cuts through the bureaucracy." He took a sip of his coffee. "Find anything?"

"The hospital started providing veterans' programs after World War II. Not like a comprehensive V.A. Hospital, but enough that most people probably didn't need to go to Johnstown or Harrisburg for routine stuff." Brent frowned, looking at the document he had open to take notes.

"Most of that is pretty standard. But about seven years ago, the hospital got a donation to expand its services to veterans—from TMQV," Brent continued. "What's really interesting is that TMQV appears to be a Russian nesting doll of shell companies with barely any documentation...but rumored to have ties with the CIA and NSA."

A shiver danced down Travis's spine. "What business is TMQV in?"

"Fingers in a lot of pies. Pharmaceuticals. Medical equipment. Imaging. Biological research," Brent replied, shooting Travis a look.

"So...not a stretch to think they might have had some medical experimentation going on? Or at least clinical trials, research projects, a little off-the-books genetic manipulation? Wait—I think I've seen this movie." Travis felt sick to his stomach.

"I can't prove that—TMQV covered its tracks like a real pro—but that's my bet. A bunch of folks here probably went off to the wars because they didn't have any other prospects and came back busted up. Good care's hard to come by—and expensive. Many of the people here might have a high school education—they're not going to be quick to question doctors, and if there are abuses, a town like this flies under the watchdogs' radar."

Travis suspected that Brent's anger was driven by his fear of CHARON and organizations like it and the Sinistram, which were willing to leave all morality behind in their quest for victory.

"If TMQV is so secretive, how do we find out what they were doing here?" Travis mentally listed possibilities.

"We look for the holes in the official records and follow the money," Brent said. "They want to call it 'veterans' programs'? Fine—I'll go through the records for that and the personnel files. I bet we can reverse engineer this to get close enough to have a good idea what was going on—and whether it's got anything to do with the deaths now."

"You don't think they would have taken their records with them?"

Brent shook his head. "The main files? Sure. But if they were hiding in plain sight, the hospital must have some record. People got paid. Staff was hired. Lab supplies and medical equipment got bought. Once we have a little more to go on, I'll call Chuck Pettis and see what his bunch of ex-CHARON malcontents might know. I need more info to be able to ask the right questions."

"We know there was a historical incident that matched Kendall and the maggots," Travis said. "Now, we've got a match with Donaldson and the miner. I'm going to go out on a limb and say that there was one or more stabbings where Becca died and that someone got crushed in a construction accident—or hammer murder—where Shelly was killed. When we match up the police records, I'll be surprised if there weren't multiple incidents spread out over enough years that people didn't see a pattern."

"Yeah, but what causes that to happen?" Brent poured himself another cup of coffee from the pot Chris brought to the table.

"Dunno—but we better figure it out fast."

The door banged open, making Travis startle. He and Brent reached for their guns before they realized the source and stopped mid-motion. A tall man in a construction worker's heavy raincoat struggled to shut the door against the wind.

"Yo, Mike. What's it like out there?" Chris hailed the newcomer.

"Not good," Mike replied. "We've gotten enough rain that there are mudslides and rock falls on some of the side roads. I wouldn't be surprised if we get a sinkhole or two before it's all said and done." Given the man's raincoat, Travis guessed he was with the county road crew or public works department.

"Is Pete back yet?" Mike asked. Travis remembered that Pete was the man who went to check on the earthen dam.

"Not to my knowledge," Chris replied. "Anyone seen Pete today?" The bar customers shook their heads or grunted negatives.

"Well, if he isn't already back, he's not going to get home on the main route. It's flooded. He'll be going the long way around—and I don't envy the drive with the weather out there."

Mike took a seat at the bar and ordered a beer. "I wouldn't be surprised if we get some power outages," he told Chris. "The wind's blowing hard enough to bring down branches. I hope folks have their generators ready."

"Liz and her gang would probably have the emergency plan activated by now, but after what happened to Shelly..."

Mike looked up. "What?"

Chris gave the short version, leaving the worst details up to the imagination. "I'm sorry," he told Mike. "I know you were classmates."

"This has to stop," Mike said.

"I think Tony's working some new leads," Chris replied and nodded toward where Travis and Brent sat. "And he brought in some outside experts."

"I don't care if Tony brings in Batman—someone's got to figure out the South Fork curse and break it." Mike took a long pull from his beer with an expression that said he wished it was something stronger.

The wind howled, and rain pelted the bar's roof. "That's it, folks," Chris announced. "We're closing early. Make sure you're good to drive—this isn't a night to push your limits."

The customers trickled out, leaving Travis and Brent alone with Chris after he sent the kitchen staff home. They put away their laptops and walked to the bar.

"Put us to work," Brent said. "I bussed tables in college. The sooner you're done here, the quicker we can all leave."

Chris gave a sigh of relief. "Thank you. That's a big help. When Mike Sokolowski thinks it's a bad night, we're already past the 'fucked up' stage."

They made quick work of the cleanup. Chris locked up behind them and turned his back against the storm. "Follow me to the house," he yelled above the wind. "It's not far."

Despite their slickers, Travis and Brent were uncomfortably damp by the time they got into the Crown Vic. They followed Chris, sometimes only able to make out his taillights given the downpour and the moonless dark.

Chris parked in the driveway of a modest post-war bungalow on a side street not far from Fisher's while Travis found a spot at the curb in front. While their host unlocked the door, Travis and Brent grabbed their bags and computers and followed him into the house.

"Thanks again for putting us up," Brent said.

"Thank you for coming out to deal with our crazy."

Chris rummaged in the fridge and emerged with beer for each of them and a plate of cheese cubes and carrot sticks. "I need a beer—and something to eat. I don't always get to finish my dinner."

They took the snacks and beer into the living room.

"Well, you've seen Fisher's. Welcome to my world. I know my neighbors way better than I'd like to. And any optimism that survived Iraq is long gone."

Brent managed a tired smile. "If that were true, you wouldn't have called us. South Fork may have bad luck, but it's got a lot of good people. They're doing courageous things—and they don't even see themselves as brave."

Chris scrubbed a hand down over his face. "I know. I'm just tired. And I understand why Father Prochazka crawled into a bottle. Bartenders hear confession every day, not just on Sundays."

"Who's Mike?" Brent asked, popping the cap on his drink and raising the bottle in a mock salute.

"We grew up together. I left and came back. He stayed. We played on the football team in high school. He's in charge of the town's road services. So if there's anyone who knows South Fork's infrastructure for good and bad, it's Mike," Chris said and took a long pull from his beer.

"Tell me about Father Prochazka," Travis said.

Chris looked surprised. "He's a guy who lost his way a long time ago and has been white knuckling it ever since. He sleepwalks through his job most of the time because this town scares the piss out of him, but I figure he's only got a year or two until retirement, and his superiors probably know about his drinking problem. Other than being soused in the evenings, he's okay. None of the hanky-panky you hear about. More like he stared into the void, and the void blinked and said 'boo,' and he's not handling it well."

"And the booze you sold him?" Brent asked.

Chris shrugged. "There isn't a State Store for twenty miles, and Father Prochazka doesn't like to drive far. I order a couple of extra bottles for him, and he pays me back."

Travis made a mental note to pay the priest a visit in the morning, wondering what had terrified him.

"You know, I'm used to customers who are bitter and angry or who've just given up," Chris said. "But after the deaths in the last couple of days, there's a fear in the folks in town I haven't felt since we were over *there*." He looked toward Brent, clearly meaning Iraq. "It's that warning in the back of my mind that things are about to get really, really bad."

———

THE NEXT MORNING, Travis woke first, padding downstairs before the others arose to make a pot of coffee and a couple of slices of toast.

Chris had left a note on the counter.

Don't wait for me—I sleep until ten most mornings. You're welcome to any food you can scrounge up. Plan on staying here for as long as you're in town. Good luck and stay safe. —Chris

Brent came down shortly after Travis, and they ate in silence, neither of them conversational before coffee. When they finished and washed their dishes, Travis shot a look at Brent. "I want to talk to Father Prochazka. I've got a hunch he knows something."

"Just drop me off at the library. Tammy is expecting me. Come join us when you're done."

The morning rain had slowed to a drizzle, but the forecast said another downpour was on the way. Travis let Brent off at the library and admired the Carnegie-era stone building with its wrought-iron fence. Then he headed for Our Lady of Tribulations, figuring the rectory wouldn't be difficult to locate.

Three blocks later, a dark, misshapen form darted across the street. Travis steered to follow it, cutting in front of a Buick that laid on the horn in protest.

This time, Travis didn't try to chase the creature on foot. He sped up, hoping to keep it in sight.

Whatever it was had a muscular, hairy body. It loped on four legs, which were longer in the back than in front. *Fuck. If I didn't know better, I'd call it a wolfman.*

The rain didn't seem to bother it, and at first, neither did Travis's pursuit. Maybe it had never been chased before. Travis didn't know what to expect as he veered down side streets and took corners too fast, hoping no pedestrians happened into his way. He expected the creature to scale a building or disappear into a storm grating at any moment.

He didn't expect it to turn to face him, rising onto two legs and baring its dangerous fangs.

Shit, shit, shit. Travis hit the brakes and threw the Crown Vic into reverse.

The creature howled and launched at the car, landing on the hood. Claws dug into the metal, and its face—with red eyes, pushed-in nose, bat-like ears, and vicious teeth—was right against the windshield, impossible to miss.

At the next intersection, Travis hit the gas, cut the wheel sharply to the right, and slewed the car in a circle. That threw the creature off the hood, and Travis jammed the car into "drive" and sped forward, right over top of where the beast had landed.

He stopped half a block away and pulled out his gun. With all the talk of "devil dogs," he'd loaded some silver bullets—just in case. Travis got out of the car, using the door as a shield until he could see the road behind him, and raised his gun.

The street was empty.

"No, no. That can't be right," Travis muttered, advancing on the stretch of pavement where the wolf-thing landed when it spun off the hood. "Where is it?"

No body, no fur, no blood, yet when he looked back at his car, he winced at the deep gouges on either side and the scratches on the hood. *I'm not losing my mind. Something made those marks on the car. But what was it? Where did it come from? And how did it disappear?*

Travis got back in his car and holstered his gun. He drove the rest of the way trying to make sense of what he'd seen and wondering if, by any stretch of the imagination, that qualified for "South Fork normal."

The small salt box-style house looked neat and tidy, with a row of trimmed bushes in front. A single rocking chair and a wooden swing decorated the front porch. Travis knocked at the door and heard a dog barking as a man's footsteps came closer.

Father Prochazka opened the door a hand's breadth. He wore a black t-shirt over jeans, no clerical collar, and his gray stubble indicated he hadn't bothered to shave yet. "Can I help you?"

"I'm Travis Dominick. I'm a friend of Chris Horvath's—he asked my partner and me to help with some of the strange goings-on lately. I'd like to talk with you."

The priest seemed to silently debate inviting him in versus shutting the door in his face. Reluctant hospitality won out. Prochazka stood to the side. "Come on in. Coffee?"

"I'd love a cup," Travis replied, hoping kitchen table talk would ensue. The dog, a terrier mix, bounced around the priest's feet and sniffed Travis thoroughly. Prochazka gestured for Travis to follow into the small galley kitchen. Travis tried to get a sense for the house without visibly looking around.

Dated but still serviceable furnishings looked cozy. Travis guessed they came with the house. Living in the rectory was part of the priest's compensation. That would explain the somewhat generic department store landscape art on the walls, decorative but impersonal. The kitchen's appliances in green and gold belonged to another era but looked in good condition and still functional. Only the dog seemed likely to belong to Prochazka himself.

"Down, Dante," the priest said, affection thick in his voice. He tossed a treat to the dog, who caught it mid-air and retreated to his bed to feast on the bounty.

"Dante—like Dante Alighieri? The guy who wrote *Dante's Inferno?*" Travis asked with a grin.

Father Prochazka shrugged. "The pup is a bit of a rascal. What can I say? I'm rather traditional." He moved to the counter, fixing their cups.

"You just missed Marjorie—she's the parish's housekeeper. Cleans the church once a week, does the shopping, leaves me fixings for breakfast and lunch, and keeps the fridge and freezer full of homemade dinners-for-one so I don't starve to death or accidentally set the place on fire trying to cook," Prochazka said in a wan attempt at humor.

He turned, carrying a hot mug of coffee in each hand, and stepped over to the table, where Travis joined him. "Sit down. Tell me what's on your mind. Excuse me for not having my collar on— despite rumors to the contrary, we really are permitted to remove it off-duty."

Travis smiled. "I understand. I was ordained...left the priesthood several years ago."

Father Prochazka raised an eyebrow. "Interesting. What do you do now?"

Travis saw no reason to lie. "I run a halfway house in Pittsburgh —and I hunt demons and monsters on my days off."

He wondered if the priest would doubt him, but the older man nodded. "So...that's why you're here. Did Chris or Tony call you in?"

"Chris, He knew my partner Brent from their Army days. He asked us to help."

"So why come here? Clearly I've been of no use ridding South Fork of its demons, real or imagined." He looked down at his coffee, and Travis read shame in his expression.

"You've been in South Fork for a while—seen things change. I don't think that the problem here is simple to fix, or someone would have taken care of it before this. I'd like to know what you've observed. Maybe we can get to the bottom of it."

Prochazka shook his head without looking up. "I have nothing to offer. Don't you think I would have done something before this if I saw a way?"

"Do you know if any of the priests in the past tried to banish ghosts or do exorcisms?" Travis knew that the average parish priest wasn't trained or—under normal circumstances—permitted to drive out demons. But nothing about South Fork qualified as "normal."

Prochazka sighed as if realizing Travis wouldn't be sent away easily. "The elderly priest who was here before me died trying to cast out an evil spirit. I received strict orders not to do something so foolish when I received this assignment."

He still didn't meet Travis's gaze. "When I first came here, I tried to follow those orders. That was twenty years ago. I was hopeful. I thought that if I took care of the parish like a regular priest, I could ease the strain and help them deal with their fears. But...it was too much. They never taught me how to minister to a haunted town. For some reason, they didn't cover that in seminary."

Actually, they did, and the unlucky ones who learned it were sent to the Sinistram. Be grateful you weren't chosen.

"Have you ever dreamed things that came true? Or seen ghosts? Anything that was difficult to explain?" Travis pressed.

"You're asking if I'm psychic?" Father Prochazka asked with a wry chuckle. "Nothing strong enough to be worthwhile." He gave a forced laugh. "My professors would say I'm not even very intuitive. But have I seen things, felt things? Yeah, enough to give me nightmares and make me cross the street or stay inside some nights. My parents wanted me to go into the priesthood, so I went. I was good at studying, but not so much the people parts of things. I guess you could say I had the head but not the heart. I stumbled through the years of homilies and weddings, funerals, and baptisms. I did what was required. Then they sent me here. Probably to get rid of me. I guess I lasted longer than they expected."

"Did people try to tell you about things they couldn't explain?"

The priest looked out the window, glancing anywhere except at Travis. "A few. Their stories scared me. I wasn't helpful and couldn't ease their fears so I gave them the 'party line'—told them they were imagining things or that the occult was against God. They went away and left me alone. I had a responsibility to help them—and I left them to struggle."

"Have you ever seen a werewolf in town—or something that might be mistaken for one?" Travis asked, taking a risk.

Prochazka's focus snapped from the window. "What do you mean?"

"Several times, my partner and I have seen shadowy creatures that look more like wolves than dogs—but not normal wolves. More like Hollywood were-creatures. We've chased them, shot at them, and on my way here, one of them attacked my car. The gashes in the metal are real. So it had to be too. But it vanished into thin air. Got any idea what I'm talking about, Father?"

The priest looked flustered. "I've heard stories. Never caught more than a glimpse myself—another reason I don't go out often at night. I told myself I was imagining things."

"But deep down, I suspect you know better."

Prochazka sighed. "There's an evil in this town that I can't explain. People talk about curses and Hellmouths and visions. I don't know what started it, but so far, no one's been able to end it, and if it doesn't fear men like you, it won't run away at the likes of me."

Travis wrestled with how much to say. "I know the Church discourages talk of demons and evil spirits—or exorcisms. But at the high levels, they believe. I was part of a Vatican group of demon-hunting priests—we were the Left Hand of the Holy Father. The Sinistram. I left because they were corrupt—but the work was real."

Prochazka stayed silent long enough that Travis wasn't sure he would respond. "So...they misled us from a truth at the very heart of heaven and hell."

"I'm sorry." Travis wasn't sure Prochazka had any illusions remaining, but he seemed to take the information to heart.

"People ask me whether I believe in God or the Devil. I've never been too sure about God, but after twenty years in South Fork, I'm positive about the Devil...or at least, the powers of darkness." He finally met Travis's gaze. "You don't have to die here. Get out while you still can."

"For the record, I don't think that what haunts South Fork has anything to do with Hell or the Devil. There are entities that feed on blood and death and suffering like we eat food. They aren't evil—they're amoral, indifferent, and hungry. Sometimes, people try to control them for their own purposes—and *that* is the true evil," Travis told him.

"It's too late for me," Father Prochazka told him. "I have been 'tried and found wanting.' I hope you can do better. But hurry. I think time is running out."

CHAPTER SIX

"I BROUGHT YOU COFFEE," Brent told Tammy when she met him in the lobby of the library. "Tried the place across the street, figured I'd bring you some since I was picking up a cup for myself."

Tammy received the takeout cup with a smile. "I will never say no to coffee." She took a sip and closed her eyes, savoring the taste. "Good stuff."

"Travis had an errand this morning, but he'll join us afterward," Brent said. They sat on a bench to drink the coffee since they couldn't carry the drinks into the main library. "We managed to come up with some interesting leads last night."

Tammy listened as Brent told her what they had discovered about the way history and tragedy—and supernatural murder—appeared to be intertwined.

"Lots of places have had terrible pasts," she said when Brent finished his story. "But they don't have the number of ongoing accidents, and they don't have spirits trying to recreate the deaths from long ago. What's different about South Fork?"

"That's what we're trying to figure out," Brent admitted. "We've got a couple of theories. There could be a natural spirit in the area—a genius loci—that somehow became twisted and malicious. Something could be attracting dangerous energies that feed on death and negative emotions. Or maybe there's a creature we haven't encountered before."

"This is what the two of you do? Hunt things?"

Brent shrugged. "We have day jobs. But, yeah. Because somebody has to do it."

Tammy gave a sad smile. "You know, that's what Tony says about being sheriff. Someone has to."

They walked into the library together. Tammy nodded in acknowledgment to the staff as they headed for the conference room she had reserved for Brent and Travis.

"What's going on over there?" Brent saw a crowd lining up to enter the community room.

Tammy grinned. "Tony's grandmother has the Sight. I asked if she would do a 'craft project' to help people make 'Dreamcatchers.' Not the Native American sort—an Italian sigil against the Evil Eye. I figure it can't hurt."

Brent chuckled. "I like the way you think."

"We've been trying to help people deal with the uncertainty. All those stories about shadow creatures snatching people have everyone on edge. We've been holding yoga and meditation classes and doing art projects to help people let go of their fears," Tammy added.

"You there! Stop where you are."

Brent reacted with alarm, hands moving toward his concealed weapon.

Tammy huffed. "Nonna—this isn't the time—"

A plump, gray-haired woman in a dark purple pantsuit barreled out of the activities room. She held a small knife and what appeared to be a half-carved lump of coal. "You." She raked her gaze top to bottom as she gave Brent the once-over. "You came. I foresaw it," she added, dropping her voice.

"Nonna Sophia—" Tammy protested.

"Hush, child," Nonna said, not unkindly. "Hmm…your partner is not quite a witch. A medium. His gift is very strong. You also have something about you that attracts the other side. Darkness has touched you, taken a toll. Death haunts you."

Her dark eyes regained their focus, and she gave a nod of approval. "Yes, I believe you will do. The old power brings what is needed." She leaned forward, stretched on tiptoe, and tapped him on the forehead. "Tell your partner to listen with his magic, see with his gift. Much is hidden here." With that, Nonna turned abruptly and headed back into the activities room, leaving Tammy and Brent staring after her.

Tammy shook her head as the doors closed behind Nonna. "Don't let her spook you. She's an amazing lady—and she really does have ability. She just approaches the world a little differently from the rest of us."

"She seems rather…intimidating," Brent admitted. "Reminds me of my grandma—who would take a ruler to your behind if she thought it would 'build character.'"

They walked on, and Tammy stopped when they reached the conference room. "I found the records you asked for—there's a lot to wade through. Gotta admit that I'm intrigued. I've been here my whole life and heard a lot of theories about why things are the way they are, but I don't ever recall seeing someone take a research-based approach to figuring out how the curse came to happen."

Brent looked into the glass-walled room, and his eyes widened at the stack of file boxes beside the large table. He reminded himself that Travis would be there soon to lend a hand and that they had narrowed down at least a few instances so they could go directly to specific dates instead of combing through everything. Still, the amount of data felt overwhelming.

"It might not be a true curse," he told her when they entered the room. "As in, whatever's going on doesn't have to be a spell cast by a witch." Brent frowned, trying to figure out a good way to explain the idea that had been knocking around in his mind.

"Have you ever been in a place with a strong echo?" he asked. "When something bad happens, it sends out an energy that can create a resonance—sort of like an echo. And when that resonance reverberates again and again, it gets stronger. That might be what's happened over the years here in South Fork—but we won't know until we do more research."

Tammy laid a hand on his arm. "Thank you. South Fork isn't your home, but you're working hard to fix it."

"Thank us if everything goes well." Brent was uncomfortable with the praise. He settled in at the table with his laptop, a pad of paper, sticky notes, and a pen. Brent set his phone nearby in case Travis called and to take photos of any useful files. Then he pulled up the addresses of the most recent attacks and studied the file boxes to figure out how the contents were organized.

Brent put a sticky note to mark where he removed a file so he could return it to the proper place. *I don't want to get my library card revoked for messing up the archives,* he thought.

His phone vibrated, and Brent recognized Chuck Pettis's number. "Hey, thanks for calling me back. I think we're running into CHARON shit, and I wanted to know if anything rings a bell."

Chuck loosed a string of creatively obscene curses before agreeing. "Sure. Hit me."

In the background, Brent could hear the tick-tock of clocks, an eccentric obsession of Pettis's. Pettis was in his fifties, formidable in a fight, and he had escaped CHARON's hold on him years ago. While Chuck hated the secretive organization even more than Brent did, he maintained a network of ties to people who kept tabs on all kinds of things that hid from the light.

"You ever hear of a Dr. Wyrick or a town called South Fork? Or a company named TMQV?"

"Ah, fuck. Fill me in. This can't be good," Pettis growled.

Brent caught him up on what they knew and provided more context to explain their questions. "Can you shed any light?"

"Unfortunately, yes," Pettis replied. The older man was gruff in his best moods, and talking about his hated former employer clearly did not make him happy. "TMQV is one of the many shell companies CHARON uses when it wants to hide its involvement. If they're around, things are already going to hell in a handbasket."

"And Wyrick?"

Pettis cleared his throat. "I don't remember that name in particular or the town you mentioned, but there was always some kind of bio-experimentation going on under the banner of 'science.'" His scathing tone left no question about his feelings.

"Every government organization tries to build a super soldier— stronger, faster, better. CHARON focused on psychic abilities and cryptids, trying to make them more powerful, easier to control, harder to kill. Whatever they say their research project is about, figure out how it could be used to get the upper hand in battle—that's what they're really doing," Pettis warned.

"Thanks." Brent rubbed his tired eyes, unsure whether confirmation from Pettis made him feel better or worse. "If you hear anything more, call me. There's something really dark going on here, and we haven't seen the worst of it yet."

Pettis promised he'd keep his ears open, and Brent took a few deep breaths before going back to his research.

Whatever Wyrick was doing, the goal was weaponization. We've just got to figure out how to defuse the bomb he left ticking.

Digging into the police records, Brent became engrossed in the town's history. He jotted notes about ideas for follow-up and added dates, names, addresses, and details to his spreadsheet whenever he found something that might be related.

"How's it going?" Travis asked from the doorway.

Brent jumped, so deep into his research that he hadn't heard the door open. "Pretty well. Wow, has it been two hours?"

Travis nodded. "I'll fill you in about my chat with Father Prochazka later—but the short version is that he believes us, although the supernatural terrifies him. I don't think we can count on him to have our backs, but I doubt that he'll work against us."

"Well, that's something at least," Brent agreed.

"What did you find?"

Brent pulled a chair over for Travis so he could easily see his screen. "It would help a lot if the records were digitized, but they aren't. I started with the newest ones and worked backward, looking for weird stuff and especially for other disturbances or deaths at the locations where the recent attacks happened."

He paused to take a drink from the water bottle in his pack. "It's slow going—I've gone back five years, but it's going to take more to see the whole picture. Still—this is what I've come up with."

Brent pointed to the spreadsheet. "I was hoping to find a pattern to the recurrences, maybe a cycle so we could predict other attacks. So far, that isn't the case, so I don't know what triggers the incidents. But some places are definitely 'unlucky.' And for a tiny town, the cops here must be run ragged, showing up to all the odd accidents, gas leaks, and wrecks. Not to mention the times people just went bonkers on themselves or others."

Travis studied the spreadsheet for a moment and caught his breath. "Yeah—that's a lot. What are the notes on the pad?"

"Ideas of other things to check at the morgue or in the newspaper files," Brent replied. "I don't think we'll be able to document every instance of the stuff that's happened here. But with both of us going through files, building enough examples to show a pattern of injuries that match historic accidents shouldn't be hard."

"From what the sheriff and Chris said, there are probably too many old injuries and deaths to predict where the next strike might be," Travis warned.

Brent shook his head. "I know. But now that I've proven that incidents repeat, we need to figure out why—and what or who is making it happen."

At noon, Tammy stuck her head in. "Come to the staff break

room. There's fresh coffee, and I ordered hoagies for you. It's raining cats and dogs, so I figured you wouldn't want to go out."

Brent stood and stretched, grateful for the break as well as the food. Tammy passed two foot-long sub sandwiches to them when they got to the kitchenette. "I guessed at what you might like—hope that Italian Club is okay. It's my favorite. There are chips too." She waved a hand toward plastic containers on a table. "Jenny brought in homemade cookies. You're welcome to help yourselves."

"I ate, so I'll leave you to it. Don't be shy on the cookies, or I'll end up eating them," she warned them with a laugh before leaving them to their lunch.

Brent was surprised at how hungry he was and made short work of the sub and chips, washing it down with unusually good coffee. Travis finished first and returned to the table with two cookies for each of them.

"Best meal I've ever eaten in a library." Brent wiped his mouth when he finished. "Too bad we can't take it out of the break room."

"A few of the libraries I used to spend time in warned that if we smudged the documents, we could end up setting off a minor apocalypse," Travis said, and Brent got the feeling he was only partly joking.

They spent the rest of the afternoon going through records, and by the time the library was ready to close, they had fleshed out the spreadsheet and added to Brent's list of notes and questions.

"I'm not sure whether we've got more questions or answers, but we've definitely got *more*," Brent said as they packed up.

"It's like dumping out the pieces of a jigsaw puzzle," Travis reassured. "At first, the pile looks impossible, but every piece you put in place makes it easy to find others, and soon the picture takes shape."

"I'll take your word for it," Brent joked. "I like word puzzles more than jigsaws."

Streetlights barely made a difference in the rain. No one was on foot—unsurprising given the miserable weather. Brent couldn't help shifting restlessly in his seat, waiting for...something.

A black form shot across the street in front of them, and in the dim glow of the lights, it looked like a person-sized, wild cat. It hissed at them and bounded off down a side street.

"Follow it!" Brent yelled.

Travis took the turn so sharply Brent held on to the armrest, but he sent the Crown Vic flying down the street after the shadow-cat. He expected it to vanish as soon as it realized they were pursuing it, but perhaps the were-cat enjoyed leading them on a chase, or hoped to turn the tables and attack because it kept going, in sight but well ahead of them.

At the end of the street, the spectral cat disappeared. Ahead lay an abandoned lumber yard.

"That's not creepy at all," Brent muttered. His head turned sharply, and then he threw open the car door. "I see it!" Armed with his heavy-duty flashlight and his shotgun, Brent ran after the creature.

"Brent! Get your ass back here!" Travis hollered. He snatched the big flashlight, turned off the car, and grabbed the flamethrower and an iron bar. "We are going to have a fucking Come-to-Jesus talk about your *enthusiasm*," he muttered as he sloshed through shallow puddles and ruts in the muddy lot.

Travis spotted the reflective lettering on the back of Brent's borrowed rain slicker. The night had turned colder, and Travis's breath clouded. The old lumberyard still had stacks of rotting wood in some places and piles of uncut logs in others.

Perfect place for an ambush.

He rounded a corner and found Brent standing in front of a slanted shelter open on three sides that still held some stacks of rough-hewn boards.

"Lost it, but I think there's something behind the wood." Brent cocked the shotgun. "Cover me."

Like there was a chance I wasn't going to. Travis edged closer, sizing up the situation. The wood was wet enough from the constant rain that the blowtorch probably wouldn't set the whole place on fire.

"Watch out!" Travis saw the were-cat out of his peripheral vision. Whether it had just appeared or had lurked in the shadows, now it perched on top of a stack of logs, ready to pounce.

The big cat lunged. Brent fired and missed.

The cat dropped to the ground and skittered behind another log pile, moving silently, toying with them. Brent caught a glimpse and fired again, getting an angry howl in response.

"Here, kitty, kitty," Travis muttered, moving to the right while Brent went left.

The were-cat jumped atop another pile of logs, and its weight sent the logs rolling. Travis and Brent jumped out of the way to avoid being flattened, and Travis loosed a fiery blast that made the creature back off, hissing and baring its fangs.

Brent sent a blast of salt to one side, forcing the were-cat to shift into the range of Travis's blowtorch.

A burst of fire caught the creature in its midsection. It yowled and twisted, glaring at Travis with golden eyes, then bucking when the rock salt from Brent's next shot hit it. The creature vanished, leaving both men glancing anxiously around.

"Where'd it go?" Brent remained ready to fire again.

"I don't think we can kill it like this, but we might have drained it," Travis guessed. He noticed that the creature's claws had dug into the woodpile where it had leapt. *At least it wasn't my car this time.*

"Shit. There are bodies. We're going to have to call the sheriff. It can definitely be solid when it wants to be," Brent replied and pointed to something on the other side of the stack. The wind shifted, and Travis caught the smell of rot.

When he turned his light, he saw two bloodied bodies that looked like they had been mauled by a wild creature. Travis swore under his breath while Brent called Calabrese.

"He's heading over," Brent reported when he ended the call. "Asked us to sit tight until he got here."

The sheriff's car showed up sooner than Travis expected, without siren or flashers. Calabrese got out and stomped across the lot.

"How the fuck did you end up here?" he asked.

Brent explained the sighting and their chase. Calabrese looked torn between admiring their courage and wanting to arrest them for stupidity.

"You fired on it and torched it, and the thing just disappeared?" Calabrese questioned. Travis took heart that the sheriff hadn't dismissed their testimony out of hand.

"These things aren't normal ghosts, but they aren't regular cryptids, either," Travis explained. "It's like they move in and out of reality."

"If I hadn't been sheriff here as long as I have, I'd think you were nuts—but unfortunately, what you're saying explains a lot. It'll be back—and it's likely not the only one," Calabrese replied.

"There are a couple of bodies behind the woodpile, in case anyone has gone missing," Brent said and beckoned for the sheriff to follow him to where the bodies lay.

"Goddamn," Calabrese muttered. "Pretty sure that's Carl Rogers and Maddie Jackson. They've been missing for a couple of days. This sucks."

"Did you find the old man who got taken by the werewolf?" Travis asked.

Calabrese shook his head. "No. We're still trying to figure out who he was." He glanced over at the damaged Crown Vic. "What happened to your car?"

"Got jumped by a wolfman," Travis replied without a hint of humor. "Mighty strange town you've got here, Sheriff."

Travis and Brent waited with Calabrese until two ambulances arrived to take the bodies. "You boys go on back to Chris's. I'll get your official statement tomorrow. No reason for all of us to freeze," he told them.

They were both quiet on the walk back to the car. Despite the rain slicker, Travis's damp clothing chafed, and water had seeped inside his boots. He turned up the heat in the Crown Vic and switched off the radio.

"You okay?" he asked Brent.

"Not really," Brent replied with a shrug. "Two more people dead, and we didn't actually stop the killer."

"They'll get a decent burial," Travis pointed out. "And we've got more 'proof of monster.' Clearly, this isn't just a mass hallucination. These creatures can be real enough to kill—and then just disappear. Now we need to figure out what the hell they are. Gotta start somewhere."

They returned to Fisher's for dinner and found the bar even more crowded than before. Brent was surprised to see Liz working with the cook to pack boxes with food.

"How are you doing?" Travis asked her.

"I'm a nurse. I deal with trauma by staying busy," she said. "Power here wasn't out long. But the storm's taken out power on the south side of town. We're moving folks who are at risk into the senior center and the library, where we've got light and heat. Chris is donating meals."

"It's no big deal," Chris said, coming over to join them. "Just helping out. Were you able to get a bus lined up?"

Liz nodded. "A tour group out of Johnstown is donating the use of a bus to take anyone who wants to go to a temporary weather shelter until the storm blows over. Some people won't leave because of pets or family, but I want to send away anyone who can go."

Brent figured it wasn't polite to agree too wholeheartedly, although he thought that getting everyone out of South Fork was smart. "That's probably a good idea."

"Does this happen often? The outages and need to evacuate?" Travis asked.

Liz sighed. "More often than it used to. The infrastructure is older, and so are the people who still live here. A lot of folks are on pensions or scraping by on Social Security. They don't have family they can go to, and this is the only home they know."

"Can we help?"

Liz looked from him to Travis. "Stop the evil. Then maybe we can rebuild our town after the storm."

Chris came around the counter and wiped his hands on his apron. "I'll help you get all that into your car. Give me the keys, and I'll back it up to the door so you don't get soaked."

Brent swallowed back a smile. *Whaddya know? I think Chris has got it bad for Liz.*

Chris returned looking bedraggled. Liz hugged him and stole a kiss. "I'll call when I get to the senior center. And I'll avoid driving through standing water. I know the drill."

"Be safe," he told her, holding her hand. "Don't take chances. What's going on—it's not normal."

Liz shot a glance at Travis and Brent. "South Fork normal, or 'other people' normal?"

"Regular normal. 'South Fork normal' is fucked up." Chris watched her go and walked to the window until the rear lights of her car disappeared in the night.

Travis elbowed Brent, a silent warning not to tease. Brent stayed silent, but his grin spoke volumes.

"Shut up." Chris snapped a bar towel at Brent.

"Didn't say a word." Brent grinned.

Chris glanced over his shoulder, but the bar patrons seemed content with their drinks for the moment. "We've been around the block a few times," he said to Brent. "We're both divorced. We've known each other all our lives. Been friends since school. Now— maybe we can find something good in this godforsaken town."

"Seriously—I'm glad for you," Brent said. "After everything, you deserve it."

The sound of breaking glass and a chair falling over made them turn, and Brent expected a bar fight.

"I said it, and I meant it," a man shouted, standing up from a table with two other men. "South Fork is cursed. There's a hunger in the darkness that won't be satisfied until we're all dead. You know it's true."

"Settle down, Harry." One of his companions reached out, and Harry threw off the restraining hand.

"I won't settle. Not this time. I tried to warn people, they say 'settle down, Harry' or 'you're imagining things, Harry.' Well, I know what I saw. I know what they did. You can look it up. But now, I'm not going to keep quiet."

"That's 'crazy' Krystyk," Chris sighed. "He gets like this sometimes." The bar owner made a move to intervene, but Brent caught him by the shoulder.

"Wait. Could we talk to him?"

Chris gave him a skeptical look. "The guy's slipped a few cogs. Everyone in town knows it."

"Maybe. Or he saw something no one else will believe—that might be true. Can't hurt."

"Be my guest. But if he takes a swing at you, don't blame me." Chris went back behind the bar. Brent led the way over to the table, where Krystyk's companions continued their effort to get him to sit down and be quiet.

The men fell silent when they walked up. "Mr. Krystyk? I'm Brent Lawson, and this is my partner, Travis Dominick. We're special investigators. Sheriff Calabrese asked us to lend a hand. We heard what you said—and we'd like to learn more."

Krystyk grinned victoriously and shot a side-eye at his nay-saying friends. "Finally. Someone who'll listen."

Brent gestured toward the back table he had started to think might as well have a plaque with their names on it. "Lead the way."

Krystyk held his head high as he strode past the other patrons, and Brent got the feeling the man was used to being the town's Cassandra.

Chris brought them coffee without being asked, and Brent wondered if it was a "thank you" for averting a scene.

"We're all ears," Brent told him. "What's this about 'hungry darkness'?"

"You're not going to make sport of me, are you?" Krystyk asked, defensive.

Travis shook his head. "No. We handle supernatural threats. We're just having some difficulty figuring out what sort of activity is going on here—or how many paranormal things are happening at once."

"Ghostbusters, huh?"

Brent chuckled. "Sort of. Nothing like on TV."

Krystyk sipped his coffee, looking pleased to be taken seriously. "I was an orderly at St. Benedict's for ten years. Ended up working with the veterans' programs because I'm ex-Army. Most of the doctors, they were legit. But this one guy, Dr. Wyrick, I didn't like."

"Why not?" Travis seemed to realize that Krystyk would need to be guided to get his story out.

"Honestly? I wasn't sure for a long time, except that he kinda raised the hair on the back of my neck, you know what I mean?" He paused to take another sip of coffee.

"I decided to keep an eye on him in case there was something hinky going on. Wyrick was all friendly and professional, but every time I saw him, I felt this *darkness*. No one else seemed to mind the guy. And at first, everything seemed to be okay."

Brent wondered if Krystyk had some untrained psychic ability, like the people Travis gathered as his Night Vigil. It would explain the man's heightened sensitivity to supernatural energy and why he sensed things no one else noticed.

Krystyk stared off into the distance as if he was looking across the years. "The other docs worked with old injuries, physical therapy, chemical exposure. Wyrick was a shrink. Maybe that's why I didn't trust him right off—that stuff wasn't real common, at least around here. He got the shell shock cases, the guys who had to drink until they blacked out to get a decent night's sleep. Like my buddy, Charlie."

When Krystyk remained quiet, Brent leaned forward. "What about Charlie?"

The older man seemed to come out of his thoughts. "Charlie and I served together. When he came home, what he saw over there did bad things to his head. So he went to Wyrick to get fixed up."

"What happened?" Brent feared that he knew, but he had to ask.

"At first, Charlie seemed to do better. But then Wyrick convinced him to do some 'clinical trials.' The trials were supposed to 'free his mind' and help him get rid of his nightmares. But little by little, Charlie changed."

"How?" Travis leaned in, encouraging Krystyk to share his concerns.

"Charlie was always an easy-going guy. Even the military didn't screw that up. Suddenly, he was hot-tempered, getting into fights. He started working out all the time when that wasn't really his thing. And then he killed someone barehanded. They said he was like a wild animal. He died in prison."

"Do you think he was possessed?" Brent asked.

"Possessed? Like by a demon?"

"What do *you* think changed Charlie?" Travis prodded.

Krystyk looked around, making sure no one was nearby and dropped his voice. "I think that Dr. Wyrick experimented on Charlie —and the other vets he treated."

"Drugs?"

Krystyk nodded. "Yes. But more than that. I think he was doing something with spirits...or at least, energies." He held up a hand. "I know it sounds insane—"

"You'd be surprised," Travis muttered.

"Part of my job was making sure the treatment areas were re-set and ready. I was helping my parents after my dad got injured, so my work schedule wasn't regular—I worked odd hours to make up for absences. There were times when I went into Wyrick's office, and I don't think he expected anyone to see what he'd been working on. I saw what I swore were spell books and Halloween-type stuff—goblets and candles and symbols I'd never seen in any medical textbook," Krystyk confided.

"I freaked out. It was like he was doing...witchcraft. Like out of a horror movie. I didn't touch anything, and I didn't tell anyone. Maybe I should have. Didn't think anyone would believe me. Maybe I half-thought Wyrick would come after me if I said something. Anyway, after that, I kept a close eye on him. I started noticing what books and papers were in his lab when I cleaned up. I went through some of the cabinets and drawers. I found where he hid things he didn't want anyone to see."

"I promise we won't judge. What do you think Wyrick was doing?" Brent asked.

Krystyk chewed his lip as if debating how much to say. Brent figured the man had been mocked for so long he hadn't expected to be taken seriously.

"Charlie told me that Wyrick was very focused on dreams. That he told Charlie to try to control them and will his dreams into reality."

"That's not so unusual—" Travis began.

Krystyk shook his head. "You don't understand. Wyrick seemed to be hung up on finding a way to make dreams *real*. Make what people *imagined* real. I found his notes and read them. He was giving the same advice to all his patients. Some of the exercises...he had them try to 'imagine' legendary creatures and bring them to life. I think...somewhere along the line, something Charlie 'imagined' took him over and destroyed his life."

Holy shit. He's talking about Wyrick trying to draw out psychic abilities using magic. This might be the lead we needed, Brent realized.

"What kinds of legendary creatures?" Travis nudged.

Krystyk shook his head. "I don't know. The whole thing freaked me out. I just remember that the notes were about dreams and fears and legends, willing things into being. I got the feeling that the people Wyrick picked to treat had some sort of ability—and he wanted to increase that talent."

Brent and Travis exchanged a look, certain that they had stumbled onto something important.

"Was there anything else that you remember?" Brent asked. "Even something minor?"

Krystyk nodded. "Back then, we still handled interoffice mail and outgoing letters. Part of my job was taking Wyrick's envelopes to the mailroom. He sent a letter every week. I remember because the address was so weird. C.H.A.R.O.N.—all capitals, like it stood for something. The address was Washington, D.C. Why did the bigwigs in the capital care about anything in South Fork?"

Krystyk took a deep breath and then drained his cup. "That's it. I've been telling people that something Wyrick did made South Fork's luck worse than usual, but no one ever believes me."

"We believe you." Travis took the man's hands in his. "What you've told us is extremely valuable. Thank you."

Krystyk looked gobsmacked. "Really?"

Travis nodded solemnly. "We need to think about what you've told us. But this was important. If you think of anything else— anything at all—please give us a call." He slid his business card across the table. Krystyk stared at the card for a moment before he pocketed it.

"Sure. Glad to help. Thanks for listening." He got up and walked back to where his companions waited, and this time, Brent swore the man had a bit of swagger in his step.

"What do you make of that?" Brent asked Travis.

"Dunno. Need to let it sink in—but I think it might be the break we've been looking for if we can figure out what it means."

Brent's phone rang, and he frowned as he answered. "Sheriff," he mouthed to Travis. "What's up?" He listened for a few moments. "Sure, we can meet you. Just tell us where." Brent repeated the address that Calabrese gave him so Travis could put it in his phone's GPS. "We're leaving now."

He looked at Chris. "Sheriff wants us to go see something. He said he's got two more situations—and they're our kind of thing. You okay if we don't make it back to close up?"

Chris nodded. "Go. I'll handle things here. See you at the house and don't worry how late—I'll be up. Watch the roads—it's bad out there."

With its broad wheelbase and low center of gravity, the Crown Vic handled well despite the bad weather. Brent looked out the passenger window, noting where lights were out and water pooled on side streets. Motion caught his eye, and for a second, he thought he saw a dark shape keeping pace with the car.

"Fuck—did you see that?"

"See what?" Travis asked, not taking his eyes from the road.

"I thought I saw another shadow creature chasing us—or racing the car. What do you think? Ghost? Black shuck? Something else?"

"Too many possibilities—not enough details," Travis muttered. "I feel like the clock is ticking faster, and we're too slow to catch up."

They had been in town for less than two days, but Brent shared his partner's impatience. "If it was easy to fix, someone would have done it by now. There has to be a piece we're missing—and if the sheriff can get us access to the autopsy records, that might be what we need to catch a break."

They parked just beyond the first responders' vehicles. Flashing lights lit the night and reflected from the dark, wet road and the alley walls. Travis and Brent got out and walked toward the cordon, and Brent breathed a sigh of relief when their "Sheriff" slickers got them past the firefighter standing guard over the alley entrance with just a wave.

"Figured you'd want to see this," Calabrese said as they joined him. He stepped back, and Brent caught his breath as he realized what he was looking at. A man was pinned against the wall on the loading dock, impaled by one of the tines of a forklift.

"Name's Kelson Reynolds," Calabrese said. "Not a bad kid, but he's been busted before for drugs. I suspect that's what he was out here to get in this weather. I've already asked for the security video."

He pointed to a camera aimed at the alley and dock. "I want to know how the hell the forklift pinned him? Why was it running? Who drove it—and why kill him? It's hardly like his habit racked up enough debt to get him murdered."

Brent noted a flicker of pain in the sheriff's eyes. "No witnesses?"

Calabrese spread his hands in a gesture of futility. "In this weather? And there aren't windows looking out on the alley. My bet is that Kelson met up with his dealer in the park that's at the end of the street and ducked into the cover of the loading area because of the rain. And then he died." He shook his head. "I don't need a medical degree to know it wasn't quick."

He turned on them with a fierce expression. "I need you to figure out what's tearing this town apart and stop it. I'm tired of burying everyone I know."

"We've got leads," Travis told him. "If we can get to the morgue records—"

"I spoke with Doc Medved. He'll make sure you can access anything you need." Calabrese closed his eyes for a moment. "Kelson isn't the only death tonight. Nora Johnson died from blood loss inside her locked house, in her bedroom, after something carved her up from the inside and left her kidneys on the mattress next to her body."

"Fuck," Travis muttered.

Brent exchanged a look with Travis and figured they were on the same wavelength. "Doc Medved works the night shift, right?"

"I'm sure he will be tonight."

"If he's okay with it, we can keep him company. That way we're around if anything odd turns up in the autopsies, and we can go through files in the meantime," Brent said. "I'll call Chris and let him know we might not be back to the house tonight."

"Being at the morgue isn't the worst way I've ever spent the night," Travis mused, and Brent decided he didn't want to know the details.

"I'll let the doc know you're on your way," Calabrese said. "And if you want to get in good with him, stop at the diner and pick up a bucket of fried chicken to go—enough for all three of you. It's his favorite."

"I think we can manage that," Travis replied.

"My nonna has the Sight—I might have a scrap of it myself," Calabrese admitted. "My intuition has always been freakishly on target. Right now, my gut is telling me to pack up and leave town, and take as many people with me as I can. I really hope you can prove me wrong."

CHAPTER SEVEN

DOC MEDVED WAS WAITING for them in the vestibule of the morgue's after-hours entrance. "Thank you for bringing food. Let's eat in the break room and talk so the food has time to settle before we go to the autopsy room. I'm still waiting for the bodies to be cleared."

They sat at the small table, and Medved brought sodas for them from the fridge. "Tony knows my weakness—the diner's fried chicken isn't good for my arteries, but it soothes the soul."

They washed down the chicken with cold Coke and enjoyed the pieces of pumpkin pie that Brent had added to the order, along with hot coffee.

"What do you hope to find in the autopsy reports?" Medved asked. "After all, I wrote nearly all of them for the past many years."

Travis cleared his throat, knowing what he was going to say sounded insane. "We've got a loose working theory that Dr. Wyrick at St. Benedict's might have been doing psychological experiments on veterans. Experiments that blended science and magic."

"Go on." Medved didn't look as freaked out as Travis expected.

"Have you ever heard of 'thought forms'?" Brent asked. "Some people refer to them as tulpa."

Travis glanced at his partner, intrigued by the suggestion. He had considered the possibility himself and found it validating that the idea occurred to Brent as well.

"Can't say that I have," Medved replied.

"I'm sure you've heard people talk about visualizing what they want and making it happen," Brent continued. "Thought forms are an extreme version of that theory. It comes out of mystic traditions, which draw from legend and old magical lore. Some people believe they can will an entity into existence and sentience—like a 'real' imaginary friend."

"I'm not sure that I follow." The way Medved held his coffee in front of his face made Travis wonder if the doctor wasn't subconsciously shielding himself from a frightening theory.

"Travis and I haven't worked out the details yet—and it's still a theory, so we need to prove it. But...what if Wyrick was using patients with latent psychic abilities to see if they could manifest imaginary creatures into reality?" Brent proposed.

"And what if his funding came from a secret government special ops group that deals with supernatural threats in some very unethical ways?" Brent continued. "So they weren't just interested in testing whether or not thought forms—tulpas—could be created. Their end goal was to *weaponize* them."

Medved's eyes widened. "That sounds like something out of the *X-Files*."

"Our lives are a lot like that—with a few other shows thrown in for good measure," Travis replied in a dry tone.

"We've looked into the history of the properties for three of the recent attacks," Brent continued. "They all echoed past events—and we believe it's likely that there were similar deaths over the years. I think Wyrick wanted to find out if the natural dark energy that's given South Fork its reputation for bad luck could be manipulated. If the government agency could do that here—and harness tulpas—then they could theoretically look for places in hot zones that had similar energies and use them in battle."

Brent sat back and shot a questioning look at Travis, who nodded his approval.

I had several of the pieces floating around in my head, but Brent pulled it together into a theory first. It's a fucking terrifying idea, but I wouldn't put something like that past CHARON—or the Sinistram.

After a few moments, Medved put down his cup. "I met Wyrick a few times. We didn't have professional reasons to run into each other, and as I recall, he kept to himself. He wasn't from South Fork—got brought in to handle the psych cases for the veterans' program. I don't remember hearing anything bad about him, but I wouldn't have said he was popular with the staff. He had an air of superiority that rubbed folks the wrong way." Medved looked from Brent to Travis. "What you're speculating—that stuff really happens?"

"We don't just stop restless ghosts," Travis said. "We've hunted and exorcised demons, handled malicious magic, and killed real monsters. So while we haven't come across anything exactly like this, we've seen things similar enough to make some educated guesses."

"This part of the state has never been heavily populated, even in its heyday," Brent said. "The forests in Central Pennsylvania are almost as wild as they were two hundred years ago. Plenty of room for creatures and natural energies to exist like they always have without being noticed. When there aren't people around, no harm's done. But when folks put down roots in the wrong place, worlds collide."

"What happened to Wyrick?" Travis asked.

Medved frowned. "He fell out of his office window in a tragic accident."

Travis and Brent exchanged a glance that spoke volumes.

Medved's fingers drummed against his coffee cup. "If you're right, how do you fix it?"

"We're working on that," Travis said. "First, we need to confirm the theory. Then we can work on reducing the danger. One step at a time."

Medved put his cup in the sink and carried the trash to the garbage.

"It could be a while before the bodies are brought over. Then it'll take me a couple of hours to autopsy each one. Might have to wait for the morning on that, depends how late they come in. I'll give you a hand looking through the reports and tell you what I remember about the weird ones."

Before they opened up the files, Medved excused himself to use the restroom, leaving them alone.

"If it were the Sinistram behind this, I'd point out that the Vatican has a long and storied history of defenestration," Travis said.

"I'm sure CHARON has pushed its share of people out windows too," Brent replied.

Medved rejoined them a few moments later, holding his phone. "Got a weather alert—and a safety warning from Public Works. More roads are washed out, and the river's rising fast. Good thing none of us are going anywhere tonight."

Medved made a fresh pot of coffee, and they sat around the conference room table with files spread out.

"The patterns are there when you know to look for them," Medved said with a sigh of resignation after an hour of searching through reports. "New deaths that are identical to old ones but with very different circumstances. I can't believe I didn't see it before."

"Don't blame yourself," Travis replied. "It's not the kind of connection that rational people expect to find."

"I knew there were strange deaths, but for a long time, there was time between them. Why do you think it changed?" Medved sounded like he still blamed himself for not noticing the connections.

"When Wyrick died, my guess is that any control he exerted over the original entity or the tulpas ended. They're acting on their own now, true to their nature," Travis replied.

His phone pinged, letting him know he had a text. A glance confirmed what he hoped. "Tammy sent me the history files that she was compiling," he told the others. "I'm going to switch over to reading these and see if we can find something useful."

They spent the next few hours working through the files. Brent and Medved whittled down the boxes of reports to a few smaller piles. Brent added details to his spreadsheet and scribbled reminders while Travis typed up his notes on his laptop.

Finally, Travis looked up. "I think the original entity was a Shubin. It's from Ukrainian lore—not surprising since many of the miners who came to this area were from that part of Europe. The legends are a little confusing. Sometimes they say a Shubin is one particular ghost, and other stories say it's a type of spirit that shows up in mining areas."

"That's one I haven't heard of," Brent said.

"My grandmother spoke of them—in the 'old world,'" Medved said. "It's a mine spirit that often appears as an old man in a fur coat who walks the deepest tunnels. The good ones warn of bad air or cave-ins. The bad ones lure miners to their deaths or set the gases on fire."

Brent leaned back in his chair and cradled his coffee. "So, it came here with the early settlers?"

Travis shrugged. "Some people believe that each hill and mountain has a spirit. Perhaps the Shubin merged with whatever land spirit was already here. Even the First People recognized that some locations had bad energy. Of course, settlers who wanted to dig coal and harvest lumber didn't care."

Brent tapped his pencil against the desk, frowning in concentration as he studied his spreadsheet. "There's a dark spirit native to this land, and immigrants bring their Shubin with them. Mining, logging, sawmills, and railroads are dangerous jobs, so there are a lot of accidents—plenty of blood."

Travis nodded. "Over time, the spirits adapt. They grow stronger from the ghosts and the death energy. And when the original industries that provided the deaths change—and medicine reduces the natural deaths, the entities are left hungry."

"Krystyk's 'hungry ghosts,'" Brent said.

"Crazy Krystyk? Seriously?" Medved protested.

"He's the one who put us on to Wyrick," Brent replied. "He might not be as crazy as everyone thinks."

"When the mining and logging and the other dangerous jobs went away, the entities needed blood," Travis continued. "They created replacements by influencing the mortality rate at the hospital and creating 'accidents' that mirrored what happened before. They're trapped in an echo."

"Then Wyrick starts poking around and not only juices up the Shubin/place spirit, he starts creating tulpas," Brent speculated.

"People created their imaginary creatures from the campfire stories they heard growing up. Their will and belief brought the tulpas into existence, but Wyrick's patients couldn't keep the tulpas under control—and neither could Wyrick," Travis picked up the speculation.

"Then the energies foraged to replenish themselves because they didn't have a master. Except—I think we're missing something big," Brent said. "There was a tipping point somewhere in there that we missed. Maybe too many people left South Fork or died, but I think somewhere in the process, the tulpas went feral and started to do whatever was necessary not to fade away."

"How do we stop them?" Medved asked with a bleak expression.

"I don't know, but I intend to find out," Travis said, resolve firming his tone.

———

JUST AFTER ONE in the morning, two ambulances pulled up with the bodies. Calabrese met them at the entrance and stood with them while the ambulance crew delivered the corpses to the morgue.

"Find anything?" Calabrese's voice sounded like a growl, hoarse from the rain and cold weather.

"We've been able to confirm pattern replication in the killings across many years," Travis said. "New deaths mimicking old ones under different circumstances. So—they're not natural."

The sheriff snorted. "There's a surprise."

Travis thought he caught a glimpse of motion in the shadows that vanished as quickly as he noticed it. "This is going to sound a little paranoid—"

"Probably not."

"More than once, Brent and I thought we saw dark shapes moving in the shadows. We didn't get a look at them, but it's happened too many times to be our imagination," Travis warned. "I don't know what they are, but it might be a good idea to call curfew and require the buddy system."

Calabrese took the information in stride. "I'd already put a curfew in effect because of the floodwater. I can add for people not to go out alone due to the possibility of mudslides and collapses."

"Any word about the dam?" Brent asked.

Calabrese shook his head. "No, and that should scare the shit out of me, but there are too many other things to worry about. The pump house itself is solid stone, so Pete can hunker down, but no word on whether he can release the pressure from the rains. He's stuck there until we can get a rescue craft to him, because we've got civilians in immediate danger."

"How are things out there?" Travis could see that Calabrese seemed to be running on empty.

"Bad. Lots of areas are flooded—this is hitting the 'hundred-year flood plain' markers. A sinkhole swallowed a car and half of the road on the main route to Johnstown, so that's closed. Lost the driver. The hole looks like it goes all the way to Hell."

Calabrese brushed his hair out of his eyes. "Liz and her pals have the senior center running an emergency shelter. Tammy is keeping the library open all night too. It never seems like there are many people left in town until you've suddenly got to find them all some-where to sleep."

Brent stepped away and returned with a hot cup of coffee, which Calabrese accepted gratefully.

"Hey—do you know anything about a Dr. Wyrick who fell out of a window at the hospital?" Travis asked. "Was there an investigation?"

"Wyrick? Yeah—but the Washington feds swooped in and took control, so we only did the preliminary investigation," Calabrese said with a note of bitterness. "Struck me as highly suspicious."

"Would there be anything in the files or evidence room related to Wyrick's death?" Travis pressed. "I know you're in the middle of an emergency, but we think Wyrick helped to bring on the supernatural activity that's causing the deaths."

"Melinda Barnes, the department's secretary, is covering the phones along with some volunteers tonight. She knows how to access the inventory system. I can ask her to see what she can find and give you a call. If homicide was ruled out, then Wyrick's case would have been closed, and personal effects returned to the family—if there were relatives," Calabrese replied.

The ambulance crew wheeled their empty gurneys back to the entrance, and Calabrese gave them a nod as they headed to their vehicles.

"I've deputized all the firefighters, EMTs, and the Public Works crew," the sheriff said. "And both of you as well—in case anyone asks. By the time this is over, I'll have half the town deputized just to keep the peace and deal with emergencies. That 'Sight' I mentioned? It's telling me that things are going to get worse before they get better. And that I should trust you. So..."

He didn't have to finish his sentence for Travis to understand the responsibility on their shoulders to figure out a way to rid the town of the energies Wyrick set loose.

"We're on it," Brent assured him.

Calabrese's phone rang, and he gave an exhausted sigh. "It's been one damn thing after another. Gotta go. I'd suggest not leaving the building until daylight. If Melinda finds that evidence box, I'll see if there are photos she can share. Stay off the street tonight."

With that, he slogged back to his Jeep, answering his phone on the way. Travis and Brent went downstairs, and a glance through the window of the autopsy room's door told him that Medved was already prepping Kelson's body.

"Nothing we can do while Doc is autopsying, so we might as well go back to the files," Travis said. "Pretty sure he'll let us know if he finds something he doesn't expect."

They refilled their coffee cups, made a fresh pot, and returned to the conference room. Brent yawned and stretched, blinking to clear the sleep from his eyes.

"Find anything interesting in what Tammy sent over? Sounds like she's going to be awake if you have any questions," Brent said as Travis sat at the table.

"She found a lot on local folklore, and it seems to tie directly into the kinds of things we're seeing. Mine disasters. Gruesome logging or sawmill injuries, and back when South Fork was in its heyday, railroad accidents," Travis replied.

"It reminds me of those stories about how the old gods wanted a blood tribute to spare the majority of villagers. Put together with the morgue records, it looks like there was a constant trickle of violent deaths over the years—fewer before Wyrick, more after he started awakening tulpas," Travis mused.

"Then the dangerous industries went away, and the entities still needed blood and death energies," Brent said. "What are you hoping to find if the sheriff has evidence from Wyrick's death?"

Travis sat back in his chair. "I don't think Wyrick died by accident, and I doubt it was suicide. That means either a rival special supernatural ops group decided he was too dangerous, or CHARON thought he knew too much. But what if Wyrick suspected he was in danger? I'm sure he had to file reports and that his minders confiscated his data. But what if he made a copy? He could have done it for insurance, blackmail—or control. If he didn't leave a trace, CHARON might have thought they got everything and missed it."

"And the sheriff wasn't looking for research notes, so they might still be in the box," Brent added.

Travis shrugged. "It's worth a shot."

Brent's phone rang. Travis glanced at the time and realized it was after two in the morning.

"Hey, Tammy. Sounds like we're all having a busy night. Mind if I put you on speaker? What's up?"

"Whenever things slow down, I do a little more digging," she said, sounding tired but energized. "Except for the whole emergency thing, researching this is the most fun I've had in a long time. And I think I've found something."

"How are things going at the library? Sheriff sounded like you had a full house," Travis asked.

"Crazy. But everyone rallied. We're calling it a slumber party. Volunteers are reading to the kids, the teens have organized their own craft projects, old folks are reading or playing cards or sleeping, and we have enough cracker packs and coffee in the staff room to tide people over for the night," Tammy replied.

"But—let me get this out before someone comes looking for me," she said. "When I researched local ghost stories and urban legends, three sites kept coming up. The Coal Miner Monument, Jonah Sanders's mansion, and St. Benedict's Hospital. I expected the old railroad tunnel to make the list, but it didn't."

"Fill us in," Brent said. "Sounds promising."

"The Coal Miner Monument has the names of all the miners who were lost in the South Fork mines over the years. There were a lot—nearly a thousand, which considering that South Fork was never that big a place even at its peak, is saying something. Cave-ins, accidents, explosions, bad air—lots of things went wrong. There have been plenty of ghost stories about the mines themselves, but the monument seems to be a focal point."

"Interesting," Travis said. "That might be useful. What did you mean about the tunnel?"

"Oh—the Conemaugh Tunnel was started when South Fork was at its peak. The mines were pumping out tons of coal, the lumber and sawmill were busy, and workers came for jobs. Jonah Sanders was the wealthiest man in town. He owned the coal mine, and he had arranged for a railroad spur from the main line to come right into town through the hills above," Tammy said.

"The tunnel had accidents and deaths during the construction. But...no track was ever run through it," Tammy continued. "The mine started to peter out, lumber prices dropped, and the rail spur idea was dropped because of cost. The tunnel was finished, but it's fenced off since it doesn't actually go anywhere."

"Under normal circumstances, I'd love to explore that," Brent admitted. "But how does it tie to the mansion?"

"Sanders lost his fortune. He wasn't popular because he made money by taking safety shortcuts that cost miners their lives," Tammy replied. "He went bankrupt, his wife left him and took their children, and he committed suicide right before he was going to be indicted for tax evasion."

"Wow," Brent said. "I can see why that might be a place with bad juju."

"And the hospital—it's always had a terrible death rate, even though many of the people who work there are very good," Tammy added defensively. "I think part of it came from the nature of a lot of the injuries—crush accidents from the mines and logging, amputations from the sawmill, burns and other bad stuff from the railroads. But...Liz can tell you that the place is haunted. There are floors no one likes to work on because they've just got bad vibes. And the fourth floor of the East wing is abandoned—too much bad history. No wonder the place is finally closing."

"That wouldn't happen to be where Dr. Wyrick had his office, would it?" Travis guessed.

Tammy caught her breath. "Yes. It is. You've spoken with Mr. Krystyk?"

"Yeah," Brent said. "Caught up to him at Fisher's. I know he sounds crazy, but we believe he's telling the truth. We've run into Wyrick's kind before."

"My mom was a nurse back when Wyrick had his program running," Tammy said, dropping her voice conspiratorially. "She didn't like the man. He was arrogant. But more than that, she thought he was callous to his patients. There were some who went missing or self-harmed. I don't think anyone missed him when he died."

"Do you know the history of the land under any of those three sites?" Travis probed. "What was there before the monument, mansion, and hospital?"

"For the hospital—that's easy. A previous hospital," Tammy replied. "There have been three of them built on that site. One burned—a lot of the patients didn't make it out. One was badly damaged from floods and had to be rebuilt. The one standing now is the third version."

Plenty of death and trauma, all on one site, Travis thought.

"And the others?" Brent pressed.

"The monument is on the spot where a strike got put down pretty brutally by the Pinkertons," Tammy said. "Fifteen men died, dozens were severely injured, and someone set off a bomb that blew up a car and killed several of the agents. It was the worst mine strike South Fork ever had."

"Which of the sites are the oldest?" Travis tried to figure out whether that could be key to unraveling the dark energy that lay at the heart of South Fork's problems. "And are there legends about any of those places being 'bad' before what happened there?"

He practically heard Tammy grin over the phone. "Oooh! Kudos to me! I thought you might ask—so I looked it up. The mansion was built on the site of another very large house, which burned to the ground after the family who lived there—wealthy merchants—came down with yellow fever and died, along with all of their servants. Rumor has it that they caught the fever on a trip to New Orleans and the locals burned the place to stop the contagion."

"Lovely," Travis said sarcastically, with a glance in Brent's direction.

"Thank you, Tammy," Brent said wholeheartedly. "This is important information. You've helped a lot."

"Really? I just followed the research rabbit hole to see where it led me," Tammy confessed. "Glad it was useful." A crash and raised voices sounded in the background. "Sorry—gotta go! Call if you need anything." Tammy ended the connection.

Travis looked at Brent. "Thoughts?"

Brent sipped his now-cold coffee. "I think we're going to have a wet, miserable, busy day. My bet is that Wyrick anchored his magic to something powerful in town, maybe a place where the original energy was already strong. We need to figure out if it's any of the sites Tammy mentioned—and if not, where else it might be. We'll have to break it to weaken the thought forms."

Travis nodded. "We also have to look at any evidence that might still be at the sheriff's. I feel certain that Wyrick hedged his bet and made a copy of his research. He'd have been a fool to believe CHARON would play straight with him. If we can find that copy, we can reverse-engineer what he did and maybe destroy the tulpas." He yawned. "And I put out a call to all our friends who know the lore for anything they've got about tulpas, Shubin, and how to get rid of them. We might get lucky."

"Do you think that either the Shubin or the tulpas can affect the weather?" Brent asked. "Because if that old earthen dam breaks, Krystyk's 'hungry ghosts' are going to have a feast—and we'll have a bloodbath."

"I've been wondering the same thing," Travis admitted. "And asking myself whether the energies are smart enough not to kill the host."

"They've never consumed more than the town could sustain before," Brent replied, catching his breath at the possibilities.

"Some creatures seem to have a built-in shut-off so they don't over-eat and kill off their food supply," Travis said. "Others gorge until everything's gone and then relocate or die."

Brent met his gaze. "This begins and ends with South Fork. We can't let it migrate."

CHAPTER EIGHT

"DANNY! WHERE ARE YOU?" *Brent shouted, scanning the park for his twin brother. They had gone to the fair, planning to gorge on junk food and go on all the rides, and when Brent turned his back, Danny had vanished.*

"Danny! This isn't funny. Where are you?" Despite the lights and music and the whir of the Ferris wheel and buzz of the Scrambler, the fair was empty. His voice echoed, and he shouted louder, starting to run.

Brent glimpsed the back of Danny's jacket as a figure went around a corner, slipping between two food trucks. Brent ran faster, but the person was gone, and then he caught sight of Danny's jacket as someone ducked into a barn. He followed.

The dark barn offered a stark contrast to the sunny summer day outside. A flicker of movement in the shadows made Brent wheel around, only to find an empty corner. The temperature dropped, and farm odors shifted to grave rot. A chill breeze thumped a loose shutter against the wall, and hanging chains jangled from the rafters.

"Danny—let's get out of here. I don't like this game. We need to go home." Brent tried to keep the fear from his voice but didn't

succeed. His heart thudded, afraid of what might have happened to Danny and terrified of what could happen to him alone in the cavernous building.

Between one breath and the next, Danny appeared on the far side of the darkened space. He looked pale and not quite solid.

"Danny? Stop joking around. Come with me, now."

"I can't—not yet. I'm trying to find my way home. Keep the lights on," Danny said, and then his image vanished.

"Danny!"

"Brent—wake up!" Travis sounded like he'd called for him more than once.

"Huh?" Brent startled, and the dream slipped away. He realized that he had fallen asleep at his laptop, leaning on his hand.

"Everything okay?" Travis maintained distance between them since shaking someone with PTSD was a good way to get punched.

"Yeah, yeah. I drifted off for a moment." Brent shook his head and blinked, then drained the rest of his cold cup of coffee. "I just..."

"You saw Danny."

Brent nodded. "Did I say something?"

Travis shrugged. "Yes, but I'd already felt his presence. It's faint and distant, but it's the first I've sensed him since he went away."

"Can you reach him?"

Travis gave him a compassionate look. "I'll keep trying. I've been sending out a call periodically since Cooper City. This is the first time I've felt him stir. Maybe he's finally regaining strength."

"Or maybe he knows we're in danger," Brent said, getting up to stretch. He glanced at the clock on the wall. "Six oh-fuck in the morning. No wonder I'm tired."

"You weren't out long," Travis said. "And you didn't snore—much," he added with a grin. Brent threw a balled-up napkin at Travis, and it bounced off the laptop.

"Did I miss anything?"

Travis was just about to answer when Medved opened the conference room door. His scrubs were clean, and the lack of blood spatter told Brent the coroner had changed after finishing his examinations.

"Well, that's done." He sounded exhausted. "They were too damn young, both of them. Awful ways to die. And...the wounds were familiar."

"More echoes?" Travis asked.

"I remembered about halfway through Kelson's autopsy about a guy who got cut in half by a snow plow about three years back. And there was another fatality before that. Similar wounds. Just as unlikely a cause."

"And Nora?" Brent asked.

"There was a surgeon back in the 1920s who killed four patients before he was caught," Medved said wearily. "He liked vivisection. So the kidneys..."

"Yeah. Matched his M.O.," Travis guessed.

Medved leaned against the wall and yawned. "That's the extent of what I learned, after five hours up to my wrists in entrails. Nights like this, I hate my job."

Travis's phone rang. "Sheriff. What've you got?"

"Video from the security camera when Kelson died. I'm going to send it over. The forklift wasn't an accident," Calabrese said. "It was driven by a ghost. And before you ask—Melinda found something in the old files. She's going to make sure that whoever is at the desk when you come knows to take you to it."

"Any photos?" Brent hoped they could get a jump on examining the contents.

"Yeah. I'll send those after the video clip," Calabrese replied. "It didn't look like much to me, but your mileage may vary. Gotta go. Let me know if you find anything essential." He ended the call, and Travis's phone pinged with the new files.

Travis pulled up the clip and held his phone so the others could watch. Even on the small screen, the grainy gray figure blinked in and out behind the wheel of the forklift. The edges of his form blurred, but no one could miss the malice in his eyes or the vicious smile as he drove the forklift forward with a jolt to impale Kelson through the gut.

"Shit," Brent muttered as Travis lowered his phone.

"That's...rough," Travis replied.

Medved shrugged, trying to play off the emotion that haunted his eyes. "After my time here in South Fork, I should be used to it. But honestly—it never gets easier."

Travis's phone pinged again, this time with photos. He sent them to his laptop, where he could make them large enough to examine in detail. "Look for anything that might conceal a backup for Wyrick's files," he told the others.

"It wouldn't be hard to hide a data card inside just about anything," Brent said. "A flash drive would be harder but still possible to conceal. And it wouldn't have to be physical media. Wyrick would have been stupid not to have backed his files up elsewhere. There could be a password, an IP address. We're going to have to go over everything carefully."

Travis stared at the pictures and the box's mundane contents. A wallet, car keys, papers, and some other odds and ends didn't look like they would hold the answer, but Brent knew valuable information could be hidden in all kinds of places. They'd need to see the box in person to find out whether it hid important secrets.

Medved glanced from Travis to Brent. "We're all beat. There are cots in the fallout shelter in the basement—I can bring them up for you to catch some sleep before you head over to the sheriff's office."

"Thanks, but I can sleep pretty well on the floor when I'm this tired," Brent replied with a wan smile. "Done it enough in the Army —and airports."

"We'll be fine," Travis assured Medved. "Just as long as we haven't run out of coffee."

Medved laughed. "That, I can promise. I order it by the case."

Brent and Travis reluctantly closed down their computers and put away their files. "I think we proved our theory," Brent said as he picked a spot to stretch out on the conference room floor. "But it sure would be nice if we knew what to do."

Travis staked out a place on the other side and blocked the door with a chair since it lacked a lock. "We'll figure it out. If it was simple or obvious, someone would have put a stop to it before now. Calabrese wouldn't have had to call in the big guns," he added with a tired laugh.

"We'd better start earning our pay then. Oh, wait. There isn't any."

"Then again, if Wyrick's research made it back to CHARON, we could be running into the tulpas elsewhere. Be nice to know how to stop them. The next ones might be worse."

"Aren't you the cheery one? Go to sleep, Travis. Catch a few hours. I suspect tomorrow will suck."

Brent wondered whether Danny would visit his dreams again, but when his phone's alarm woke him three hours later, he knew his brother had not returned. Sadness swept over him, fresh grief at a new level of loss. Danny's ghost had been a companion for so long that its absence in the months since Cooper City had awakened the feelings he thought were settled long ago.

"No word from Danny?" Travis sat up, stretching and twisting.

Brent shook his head. "I knew it was a long shot but—"

"You miss him," Travis replied as if hanging out with a ghostly brother was perfectly normal. "And grief's a cycle, not a straight line. If he can come back to you, he will. The odds are looking better than they were just days ago."

"I know. And given everything going on, it's the least of our problems."

Medved came to the door, looking annoyingly chipper. "Coffee's nearly done, and I've got peanut butter and crackers. Not fancy, but better than nothing. If you want a shower, there's a no-frills one off the autopsy room. Help yourselves."

Travis opted to eat first while Brent went to clean up. He grimaced at the state of his clothing as he stripped it off but knew there was no chance of getting back to their bags at Chris's house until they had chased down the leads they discovered during the night. He tried not to let the pressure get to him, but Brent shared Calabrese's gut instinct that time was running out.

Travis headed for the shower as soon as Brent returned to the break room and took his partner's spot at the small table across from Medved.

"Do you pull all-nighters often?" he asked as the doctor put a plate of crackers and a jar of peanut butter in front of him.

"More than I should at my age," Medved replied. "Blame it on South Fork. It's not like the dead are in a hurry, but families want answers, and evidence degrades. Whatever nasty spirits cause the havoc in this town seem to like the night. Somehow the bad stuff rarely happens during daylight hours." He crossed himself reflexively as if he realized he just tempted fate.

Brent's phone rang, and he recognized Chris's number. "Everything okay?" he asked, worried.

"Even for South Fork, things are fucked up," Chris replied. "I'm going to open the bar early for people who don't have anywhere else to go. Power's out in a lot of places. The storm took down wires, and no one's coming to fix that real soon. Liz says the library is at capacity —they've even got people in the old fallout shelter in the basement and the librarian's apartment on the third floor that hasn't been used in forever."

"Travis and I think we're getting a bead on the problem," Brent reported. "We'll be chasing down some new leads now."

"Be careful out there," Chris warned. "Two more people have gone missing. Maybe it's floodwaters. But folks have been reporting creatures in the shadows. It's insane—people think they see all kinds of things, but that doesn't change the fact that we can't find two people."

Fuck—that's two more on top of the old man and the bodies we found at the lumber yard. This just keeps getting worse.

"Noted. Thanks for the tip. And it's possible that the things we're hunting can change form depending on who's looking at them," Brent said, figuring that tulpas might take shape based on the fears of the closest individuals. *Are they fixed or fluid? Do they arise from a single memory, or are they a composite?*

"Well, fuck. That can't be good."

"We're working on the solution," Brent assured him, trying to sound more positive than he felt. "Stay in touch—and keep people indoors."

"We've got enough beer to last for quite a while," Chris replied with strained humor. "Go live up to your reputation."

Brent put his phone back in his pocket and finished his coffee, then washed out his cup. "Thanks for letting us crash here," he told Medved. "We're going to follow up on some leads we found earlier. Out of curiosity, do you know if Wyrick was autopsied? Or what happened to the body?"

Medved gulped his coffee and then poured himself another. "Yes to both. I did the autopsy. The cause of death was traumatic injuries from his fall. No evidence of drugs or intoxication, and the sheriff found no reason for suspicion of foul play. Also no suicide note; so it was ruled accidental. That's always bothered me because while I couldn't prove otherwise, it never seemed right."

"Why?" Brent leaned back against the counter.

"Because of the height of the windowsill. I couldn't see how someone could fall out of that window 'by accident.' But there were no witnesses, no reason to think someone had been with him when it happened, so I kept my thoughts to myself," Medved said.

"And the body?"

"Some guys in dark suits came and packed up everything in his office and lab, including the equipment. They arranged for his casket to be shipped to wherever they took the rest of the stuff. Somewhere near Washington, D.C., I think."

"Langley?"

Medved nodded. "Yeah, that sounds right."

"Shit. That's Spook territory—the *other* kind, CIA. Seems a bit 'convenient' for Wyrick to have family in that area." He swore under his breath. "Do you know what happened to Wyrick's patients?"

"Only from hearsay—nothing official. I wasn't keeping track, but I'd catch the gossip. Small town, everyone knows everyone. And of course, a lot of people don't like to talk about seeing a psychologist, so I didn't know who all might have been a patient. But—" Medved drained his cup.

"Two committed suicide. Three had mental breakdowns. It gets murky on some of the others. They died younger than the average lifespan, but so do a lot of people in Central Pennsylvania. So was it something Wyrick did, or the general pollution exposure, crappy health insurance, and slate of chronic conditions that are way too common in these parts?"

"The feds took all of Wyrick's hospital records. Wouldn't there have been some other groups keeping track? The V.A.? Insurance? Medicare?"

"Maybe—but getting to that information won't be fast or easy. Lots of layers to go through. And I thought I heard something about the hospital offering Wyrick's program free to veterans. That would have been quite an incentive if Wyrick wanted to recruit patients. Folks around here don't have much cash," Medved replied.

Brent mentally added tracking down Wyrick's patients to his to-do list. Travis came back from his shower and raised an eyebrow, questioning the conversation he missed.

"Ready to go? We might need to swim. It's really coming down out there," Brent said, figuring he'd fill Travis in while they drove.

"I forgot our water wings," Travis joked. "We'll have to doggy paddle."

They thanked Medved again and headed out.

"Which one first?" Brent asked.

"Let's start with the least likely, and end up at Wyrick's floor and the sheriff's office." Travis pulled out onto the street, wipers barely keeping up with the rain.

"Sounds like a plan. Have you figured out what we're supposed to find?"

"Hoping we'll know it when we see it."

It didn't take long to get anywhere in South Fork, and minutes later, Travis pulled up in front of the Miner's Memorial. The rain eased off a bit, but they still needed their slickers when they got out of the car, and Brent knew that they'd be soaked by the end of the night.

The large gray granite rectangle looked like an oversized tombstone. Some of the miners who died on the job were probably buried in the two cemeteries, but for others whose bodies were never recovered, the monument was their only remembrance.

"There are a lot of names," Travis observed, taking in the carefully inscribed rows. "I knew mining was dangerous but..."

"Owners who cut corners on safety made it more so," Brent finished for him. "I've read about superintendents cutting into the support pillars to eke out a bit more coal or skimping on maintenance for the fans that pulled the bad air out of the mines. Some of the disasters could have been prevented if it weren't for greed."

Travis closed his eyes and rested a hand against the rougher granite of the monument's corner. Brent guessed his partner was checking for ghosts or trying to get a psychic read on the marker's energies.

A few minutes later, Travis opened his eyes. "The ghosts who cling to this place aren't our problem. They're victims, not perpetrators." Travis raised his hands, palms out, and said a blessing to ease the passage of those ghosts who wanted to move on.

Brent watched, on alert for an attack. He trusted Travis to deal with the spirits, but an uneasiness remained that Brent felt sure wasn't linked to the revenants. He had learned years ago to trust his gut, so he turned slowly, scanning for danger.

Dark clouds made it feel much later than the actual time. Brent eyed the shadowed places beneath trees and near buildings, unable to shake his certainty that something was watching them.

He pulled out his shotgun from beneath his raincoat and chambered a salt round. Travis was still deep in his connection to the departing spirits. So when Brent saw the slow lengthening of darkness behind the monument, he pivoted and drew down on it.

In a single heartbeat, the shadow changed, legs emerging from a muscled, furred body, head and neck coming into focus as the hellhound took shape.

Brent fired as Travis spoke the last words of his litany.

"Run!" Brent pushed Travis ahead of him while trying not to turn his back on the all-too-solid-looking creature behind them.

Brent heard the shadow monster growl and could smell the sulfur on its breath. He got off another shot, and the hellhound slowed but did not stop, and although the salt hit it square in the face, the sharp crystals raised no blood or ichor.

Great. I can't hurt it—but I bet it can hurt me.

As if it guessed his thoughts, the monster swiped at him with a wide paw. Brent bit back a cry of pain as sharp claws ripped through his jeans below the knee and dug into his flesh.

Travis grabbed him by the shoulder and shoved Brent behind him, dousing the demon dog with salted holy water from a flask in his pocket. That bought them a few precious seconds, enough for Travis to half-shove/half-carry Brent into a garden bed surrounded by an ornamental iron fence.

"By all that is holy, I abjure thee," Travis shouted. "And I refuse to believe you have power here. Be gone!"

The hellhound vanished, and Brent slumped against the lone tree in the center of the plantings. The creature that pursued them might not have been "real," but the gashes and blood on Brent's leg and his torn jeans certainly were.

"Do you think it'll come back?" He panted, still gripping his shotgun.

Travis eyed the area around them for another minute, then shook his head. "Not quickly." He turned to Brent and saw the blood. "Fuck. He got you."

"I'm okay," Brent said through gritted teeth. "It's not deep."

"Bullshit. You're bleeding. Let's get back to the car. I can patch you up and decide what to do after that."

Brent resigned himself to leaning on Travis as he limped back to the Crown Vic. Neither ghosts nor devil dogs harried them, and the heavy rain meant no one else was in the park to question his injury.

Travis drove them to a defunct gas station with a protective overhang above the useless vintage pumps. It sheltered them from the worst of the storm, although gusts still drove the rain sideways now and again.

Travis got the medical bag from the trunk, a far more specialized and comprehensive kit than its civilian counterpart. Brent swiveled in the passenger seat so that he could put his legs outside the car, and Travis squatted to have a look.

"You were lucky. They're not deep enough for stitches and not long enough to hobble you, but damn—it could have been a lot worse." Travis worked as he talked, dousing the gashes with holy water and then antiseptic, following up with an ointment made from ingredients known to repel both infection and magical taint. It hurt, and Brent bit his lip to keep from crying out.

"If you hadn't slowed it down with the rock salt...if we didn't know to get inside the iron fence...that thing could have had you for puppy chow," Travis fretted as he closed the worst of the cuts with a butterfly bandage and then bound up the leg with gauze.

"You think it was a tulpa?"

"Don't you?"

Brent nodded. "Which means they're clearly solid—and capable of killing. So regardless of what the others might look like to their victims, I think we know what took the people who disappeared and what happened to them."

Travis stood and packed supplies back in the med bag, then offered Brent an antibiotic and something for pain, along with a bottle of water to swallow them down. "You want to go back to Horvath's and rest?"

Brent shook his head. "I don't think we can afford the time. Let's head for the mansion. By the time we get there, the pills will kick in."

Travis looked skeptical but nodded. "All right. But if you start to get a reaction—"

"You'll be the first to know."

They drove to the Sanders mansion and stayed in the car for an extra moment, viewing the grand house. "Knowing what we do, it almost feels like Mob money, looking at how wealthy Sanders got when his mines were death traps for the workers."

"That could certainly create a well of negative energy," Travis agreed. "It's a museum now—no one's lived there for a while. Let's see if we find anything important."

Sanders's home was an ornate, sprawling Victorian that took up the entire block. Given the modest homes Brent had seen around town, the opulence of Sanders's house was even more ostentatious.

"You know that the coal companies built housing for the miners, but it trapped them into owing their rent to the mine landlord. They bought supplies at the company store and basically paid their salary back—and more," Brent said.

"Plenty of reason for angry ghosts—especially the miners who died," Travis remarked. "Let's go see what we can pick up on."

Thanks to the weather, the normally scheduled estate tours were canceled. Travis and Brent picked the lock on the back door and moved cautiously through the space. They looked closely at the furnishings, decorations, artwork, and personal possessions preserved in the house, trying to sense any supernatural energies.

Brent felt a pang, wishing Danny's ghost was with them. Danny had been good at running interference with other spirits and some-times cajoling a fellow revenant into sharing information or discovering information hidden from mortal eyes. The silence when he reached out for his twin's presence hurt.

The focused look on Travis's face told Brent that his partner was probably trying to sense whether demons had left behind any tell-tale evidence or if he could pick up traces of dark magic.

"There's an old shadow here, but it's not one of the usual culprits," Travis remarked. "Like a stain that won't come out. There's no malicious haunting. A few ghosts who don't want to move on, but nothing dangerous. They're more forlorn than anything."

While the old house was an interesting piece of history, nothing appeared to be related to the Shubin or the energies attacking the town.

"Well, that was a bust." Brent limped back to the car and dropped into the passenger seat of the Crown Vic.

Travis called Liz to let her know they were on their way to St. Benedict's so her contact would know to expect them.

Beth, a tall thin nurse with short gray hair, was waiting for them in the lobby and held out two visitor's passes.

"I can take you up to the fourth floor, even though it's not being used for patients now," Beth told them as they followed her. "We'll have to get off the elevator on three and take the stairs." She shivered, even though the hospital was a comfortable temperature.

"I get the feeling the fourth floor isn't a popular place," Brent remarked.

He could almost see the emotions war in Beth's expression, struggling between fear and professionalism.

"No, it's not. Hospitals are perfect haunting grounds because even at our best, people die. St. Benedict's has a checkered history. Some bad things happened here, and there were some bad people. Four has an...energy...that gives folks the heebie-jeebies."

"Energy?" Travis asked as they exited the elevator and wound around to a stairwell.

"You'll feel it. Everyone does. When the floor was in use, staff fought not to get assigned to it. Lots of turnover. And it wasn't just our imaginations—outcomes on four were worse than elsewhere. We were all glad to see it close."

Brent felt a frisson of unease when Beth unlocked the door, and they stepped into the fourth-floor corridor. *She wasn't kidding about energies. This place has bad juju.*

"Liz said you were interested in Dr. Wyrick's area. It's over here. Just—be quick. I have to stay with you because no one's allowed here unchaperoned, but I'd really rather be anywhere else," Beth confessed.

"Thank you," Travis told her. "I promise we won't take long."

Travis's pinched expression made Brent wonder what his partner experienced from four's psychic hangover. The maintenance-level lighting accentuated the floor's abandoned state, adding a feeling of melancholy.

"I don't imagine there's anything to find," Travis said. "Feds probably picked it clean."

Beth nodded. "I remember when that happened—his accident and all. Terrible thing. But it was almost like in those movies where the black SUVs show up, and guys in suits with earpieces and sunglasses walked in like they owned the place, bossed everyone around, packed up everything, and left. All they were missing were the helicopters," she added, sounding a bit unnerved.

Wyrick's program had been given a suite of rooms with a waiting area, consultation space, and what had probably been an office or storage area. Nothing about the furnishings looked unusual, and the same drab white paint made the area unremarkable.

"Not much to see," Travis mused, opening and closing empty filing drawers.

Brent eyed the window where Wyrick had taken his fatal fall, staying well back. He felt a headache coming on, and the desire to leave felt like a persistent itch, more urgent by the moment. "Are you picking up on anything?" he asked Travis.

"There's bad energy here, but the ghosts are keeping their distance. I don't think they like this place any better than we do." Travis sounded distracted as he made a thorough search.

"You can see ghosts?" Beth's voice rose to an almost squeak.

Travis nodded. "Yeah. Don't worry—they aren't dangerous. They just don't want to move on." Travis covered his face with his hands, muffling a cry of pain as he sank to one knee. Brent moved to help and realized that it wasn't a migraine—it was a vision.

"Travis!" Brent gripped Travis by the shoulders, gently shaking him loose from the horrors only he could see.

"Should I call someone?" Beth sounded frightened.

"No! He'll be okay. It's just a vision." Brent told her without taking his worried gaze off Travis.

"I'm all right," Travis forced out. "Just...give me a minute."

"You got this?" Brent's voice dropped so only Travis could hear.

"Just like always."

"Then we are so screwed." Brent managed an encouraging half-smile.

Travis got to his feet. Beth walked a lot faster leaving than she had on their way in, locking the door behind them when they made it back to the stairwell without complications.

Travis stayed quiet as Beth led them to the main lobby. Brent made small talk, trying to keep from freaking out. They thanked Beth and headed back to the car.

When they got to the Crown Vic, Brent insisted on driving. He handed Travis an energy bar and a bottle of water from a bag in the back. "Want to talk about it?"

Travis gobbled the bar and gulped the water before answering. "I got a glimpse of how things were when Wyrick was still alive. Bland, institutional office. Wyrick looked like he was in his forties, with cold eyes."

He rubbed his temples. Brent reached for the ibuprofen and offered a couple of tablets along with another bottle of water, which Travis accepted gratefully.

"There was a guy sitting on the couch—a patient," Travis went on. "He looked like he was under a spell or in a trance—and terrified. Black shadows slithered all around him, circling the couch. Maybe that's what a tulpa looks like before it's been shaped by someone's fear. So much dark energy. Malice. And raw hunger."

Travis shivered, despite the car pumping out heat full blast.

He called the shadow creatures, Brent thought. *And now they won't leave.*

Brent put the car in gear. "Next stop—the sheriff's office and the box."

"Okay," Travis replied. He was silent for a few moments. "Wyrick was using his patients to conjure the shadow creatures. I think our tulpa theory is right, and he found a way to soup them up just like he did the Shubin."

"That might explain why the ghosts kept clear," Brent replied as he pulled out of the lot. "Maybe we'll find what we need in the box. We're missing pieces of the puzzle—and running out of time to find them."

———

MELINDA at the sheriff's office just nodded when they identified themselves. She had a pleasant face, with lively blue eyes and a tired smile. Her long dark hair was pulled back in a ponytail, and Brent figured she might be in her early forties.

"I've been expecting you. Right this way." She led them to a locked interrogation room and opened the door.

"Don't add or take anything, and don't alter anything. The sheriff approved photos. If you think something really needs to leave the room, he has to okay it."

None of the rules surprised them. "Can do," Travis assured her. "Thank you very much."

The banker's box bore an identification sticker and a bar code. The seal had been broken when Melinda opened it the previous evening. Since Wyrick's case had been ruled accidental, it wasn't likely civil authorities would care much about what happened to this leftover collection of items.

"How do you think CHARON missed this?" Brent eyed the box as if it might bite.

"It might not have occurred to them that the local cops would investigate in much detail," Travis replied. "The Washington crowd usually thinks everyone outside the Beltway is too stupid to live."

"You're not wrong."

Travis held his hand over the box and paused before touching anything, and Brent knew his partner was sensing for magical traps or residue. "It's clean," he finally said and lifted the lid.

They peered inside. Brent recognized several of the items from the photo, a mundane collection of personal possessions gathered with no thought to anything supernatural. It didn't take long to spread the contents out on the table. A slim wallet/money clip, watch, ring, upscale pen, and a few handwritten notes on scrap paper looked like they had been the contents of Wyrick's pockets. A thin manila folder and a day planner lay in the bottom of the box.

"All right, let's see what we can find," Brent muttered. He reached for the planner while Travis took the folder. Brent scanned the entries, unsure of what to expect.

"Keeping a written day book seems kinda old school," he said as he tried to decipher Wyrick's handwriting. "Unless there was a reason he didn't want the information online?"

Travis looked thoughtful. "There are reasons people keep a 'dumb computer'—one that is never connected to the internet so it can't be compromised. This could be the low-tech version."

"And the government guys didn't realize it was missing because it wasn't what they'd have been looking for." Brent flipped a page. "This looks like an appointment book. He used initials, but the sheriff could probably figure out who's who. If there's anything about what they did in their sessions, it looks like it was written in code."

Travis shuffled the papers in the folder. "There are lists of common fears. Some of them have initials next to them. Don't know if those fears were suggested by patients or were ones he created for them."

Brent reached for the watch and ring while Travis pulled the notes toward him. Brent took the back off the watch, looking for any hidden additions. Then he examined the ring, poking at it to see if the stone came out, looking for inscriptions. "Nothing."

Travis shook his head. "The notes are either a brilliant code, or they really are his grocery list and a reminder to pick up his dry cleaning."

That left the money clip and an assortment of odds and ends that might have been on top of Wyrick's desk.

"None of this looks important," Travis said, annoyed. "Maybe Wyrick was a super-spy. If so, he's got me baffled."

Brent turned the slim wallet back and forth. He removed the couple of folded twenties from the clip and examined the driver's license and credit card held on the other side.

"Brent?"

He ignored his partner and focused on the clip, flipping it backward. Tacked to the back of the clip was a SIM card.

"Bingo," Brent muttered, holding up his prize.

Travis eyed the card as if it were a snake. "We need to read that— and we need to send it to the Alliance."

"Yeah—I think that would be a real good idea." Brent took the back off his phone case and switched out his card for Wyrick's, letting it load.

"You know, we don't have any idea what's on there. You might have just sent nuclear codes." Travis sounded like he was only half joking.

"I guess we'll find out pretty quick if I did."

Travis came to stand behind him, looking at the information as Brent scrolled through. "Shit—it's going to take a while to figure out what's here."

"That's why I'm sending it to Simon Kincaide with an SOS. There may not be anything in this to put the genie back in the box. Wyrick super-powered a Shubin and made tulpas real. Did he know how to stop them? Was that something he was interested in finding out?" Brent asked.

He made sure that a copy of the information was saved on his device, then uploaded to a secure server and sent an encrypted email to Simon, along with a plea for help. When he was certain the message had gone through, he removed the card, replaced his own, and put Wyrick's back where he found it.

"That's a hot potato to leave with the local cops," Travis said.

"No one's thought to look for it in six months. If someone gets to you and me, it's the first thing they'll look for," Brent replied.

That's assuming we get out of South Fork alive.

Melinda came to the door and leaned in. "How's it going? Find what you need?"

"Maybe," Brent answered, not wanting to lie. "Is the sheriff around?"

She gave a brittle laugh. "Not hardly. We've got three missing people, reports of those freaky shadow things all over town, the river's rising, and there's a jack-knifed truck blocking the main highway— and a partridge in a pear tree."

"Are you from South Fork?" Travis asked her.

"Born and bred. Not much to brag about, but I'm a hometown girl," Melinda answered with a flip of her ponytail.

"We have a theory that Wyrick was using his patients' fears to make those shadow things and bring them into existence," Brent told her, taking the chance that she wouldn't just laugh and walk away. "He recorded his patient appointments in his day book, but he only used initials. The feds took all his records. If you looked at the initials, do you think you could guess who they were? Knowing that he targeted veterans might narrow it down."

Melinda frowned, probably debating the legality of their request. "Why do you want to know?"

"We're trying to un-do what Wyrick did before the energies he created hurt more people. The stronger they get, the harder they'll be to stop," Travis told her. "We'd like to talk to them and see if we can get some insight into what Wyrick did."

"They might not want to talk about it. He was their therapist," she pointed out.

"That's their right. But I don't think they ever signed up for bringing killer, imaginary friends to life and setting them loose on the town," Brent said.

"I'll give it a shot," Melinda said. "No guarantees. Believe it or not, South Fork may be small, but we don't all know one another."

"I believe in you," Brent said with a grin.

"Flatterer," Melinda tossed back with a smile. "I'll do my best."

Travis and Melinda took the day book to the front desk while Brent stayed behind to put the contents back in the box and study a little of Wyrick's download.

His phone rang, startling him out of his concentration. "Hey, Tammy! What have you found for us?"

"You know we've got half the town holed up here, right? I figured I'd crowdsource information," Tammy replied, sounding chuffed over whatever she had discovered. "I got the knitting circle to tell me the ghost stories and local legends they had heard. And did I get an earful!"

Tammy chuckled. "Turns out that when a disaster is about to happen, people report seeing an old man in a dirty fur coat walking back and forth in the distance before he vanishes. The ladies who told me were all in their seventies, and they swore they had heard that story as children from their grandmothers."

"The Shubin," Brent murmured. "Except it doesn't warn people about danger—we think it might have a hand in causing it."

"I know—creepy, isn't it?" Tammy seemed to be enjoying her research. "The teenagers had a different legend. They said people have seen an angry thin man in a white coat staring down from a window on the fourth floor of the hospital, but that's the closed-off wing—no one's supposed to be there."

"Wyrick."

"Could be. Also heard a lot of stories about seeing those shadowy whatsits, the sneaks. Seemed like everyone had a story of either seeing one themselves or knowing someone who did. And they all think the sneaks are the reason people have gone missing," she reported.

"I've got to agree with them on that one," Brent said. "Are you safe at the library?"

"Oh, yeah," Tammy assured him. "The building is solid as a rock, and we've got a wrought iron fence around it—keeps out the bad ghosts. And three people said they saw Miss Liddie, so she's on patrol."

"Miss Liddie?" Brent welcomed Tammy's help, although her casual acceptance of his weird supernatural theories still surprised him.

"Miss Elizabeth—Liddie—Townsend. South Fork's first librarian. Died a hundred years ago. She started the library when the town was first founded, went to Pittsburgh to see Andrew Carnegie himself to ask him to build one of his libraries here, and tirelessly knocked on the doors of local businesses to get money for books. She's buried with a book-shaped headstone behind the library. There's a little memorial garden with benches for people to sit and read—it's a real nice place."

"And there've been sightings?"

"Oh, yes. Whenever South Fork is going through a rough patch, people report seeing Miss Liddie in the library. She's kind of like our guardian angel. She was tiny but fierce," Tammy said proudly. "One time, one of those holy rollers came in and raised a fuss over romance books, and she pushed him onto a book cart and wheeled him out of the building—sent him rolling down the road if you can believe the story!"

"There are tales about her alerting librarians to wiring problems that avoided fires, or roof leaks, or anything that threatens 'her' library," Tammy continued. "So, it's a good thing if she's watching over us."

Brent had never relied on an assist from spectral librarians, but given the situation, he'd take all the help they could get. "How did the amulet-making session go?"

"Like a charm," Tammy replied with a snicker. "Tony's nonna is an impressive woman. Half the town thinks she can put the Evil Eye on them, and the other half wants her to tell their fortune. We've got enough 'dreamcatchers' hanging all over the library to scare off all the bad ghosts in the county!"

"We also had people draw their fears," she added. "It seemed to fit with your tulpa idea. Aimee, our yoga guru, is doing a session to help people focus on their drawings and release their anxiety. I figured it couldn't hurt."

"Good work," Brent replied.

"Nonna had a message for you." Tammy's words snapped Brent to attention.

"For me?"

"For you or Travis. Nonna says she has a special 'working' that she's saved for when this day would come." Tammy sighed. "I know that sounds overly dramatic, but that's an exact quote. Nonna is very old world."

"No, no. That's totally okay," Brent assured her. "Old world might be what we need. We'll swing by."

"Be prepared that she might want to talk to you when you get here." Tammy paused. "I know she can seem a little...odd. But I do believe Nonna has the Sight. If she tells you something, it's worth your while to listen."

"I'll take that to heart," Brent said sincerely. "All your information is fantastic. But I have one more request."

"Shoot," she said, sounding excited for a new challenge.

"Do you happen to have any maps for the mines? Especially the oldest ones? I'm working on a theory about where some of the dark energy has been all these years, and the mines are a natural location."

"If this darkness is in the mines, it could go anywhere in town. That would be worse than being in the drinking water. There are mines underneath all of South Fork. I'm pretty sure the oldest, deepest mine runs under what's now the hospital, the Miner Monument, and the mansion. Got maps for some of the mines, but not sure about having maps for all of them. The record-keeping was fast and loose back in the days before OSHA," Tammy told him.

"I know. But still—please try. It could be important."

"I'm on it," she promised. "Gives me a reason to escape the madness for a little while and hide in the special collections room. Let me see what I can find."

Tammy ended the call. Brent glared at the box full of Wyrick's stuff as if that might force the confession of its secrets. Then he sighed and put the top back on. Brent walked out to where Melinda and Travis were talking at the front desk.

"Melinda is going to try to figure out who the initials refer to and contact them to see if they'd be willing to talk to us," Travis explained. "That keeps confidentiality, but it also makes the connection."

"I'll tell them to meet you at Fisher's at six," Melinda replied. "They're probably regulars there, anyhow."

"Much obliged—for everything," Brent said.

"Keep an eye out for the shadowy things," Melinda warned. "The sneaks. Got another missing person report—fourth one in twenty-four hours. Might turn out some people got carried off in the flooding, but every report mentioned creepy shadows. So, watch your backs."

"We definitely will," Travis told her. They headed for the Crown Vic, avoiding the worst puddles, resigned to the steady downpour.

"Where to now?" Brent asked as the big engine rumbled and the wipers started their *thwack-thwack* rhythm.

"Back to Fisher's—after a stop at the hardware store for some big bags of rock salt," Travis said. "The library has Miss Liddie's ghost and the iron fence. Maybe we can talk Mike Sokolowski into spreading road salt around the community center. But we know Fisher's is a gathering place, and we can do our best to protect it."

Brent nodded. "What about the people getting taken by the tulpas?"

"The best thing we can do is figure out how to dispel the tulpas and bind the Shubin. Much as I'd like to get the road crews out with salt trucks, they can't go everywhere, the rain'll just wash it away, and the drivers are needed elsewhere," Travis admitted.

A tall woman with long, dark hair eyed their cart that was piled high with fifty-pound bags of salt and a dozen pieces of iron rebar.

"We met at Liz's house the night Shelly died. I'm Jamie Kerr. I own this joint."

"I remember," Brent replied.

"We're hoping you can figure out how to stop what's going on. No pressure," Jamie said. "What's all this for?"

"Most spirit creatures are repelled by salt and iron," Travis explained. "We don't know for sure if the tulpas—the sneaks—will be, but odds are good it'll slow them down. We'll line the doors and windows at Fisher's with salt, and we've got the rebar in case we need to fight our way clear of the creatures."

"Tulpas? That's what the shadow things are?" Jamie looked intrigued, not skeptical.

"That's what matches the lore best," Brent replied. "Someone called them here, and we need to make them leave."

"I can send Mac with a load of bags and rods over to the library and community center," Jamie mused. "Liz and Tammy could use the help. You got any more do-it-yourself ghost busting ideas? I'm all ears."

"Shotgun shells filled with rock salt work good on ghosts," Travis volunteered. "Iron nails or iron pellets work too—just need to make sure people aren't in the line of fire."

"Shotguns and pipe bombs. Got it," Jamie replied, and the grim set of her mouth suggested she took them seriously.

"Hopefully, it won't come to that," Brent said.

"South Fork isn't a lucky place," Jamie told him, waving off Travis's credit card when he tried to pay. "So smart people prepare for the worst. Keep your money—this one's on the house."

———

FISHER'S PACKED parking lot confirmed that South Fork locals deemed it a safe place. The neon window signs reflected on the wet cars, and the mist gave the glow a creepy nimbus. Travis pulled up to the back door as Brent gave Chris a call and explained their cargo.

"You want to do what with this now?" Chris gave them a skeptical look as he helped them unload.

Brent explained the process and the effect on spirits. "We're narrowing in on how to get rid of them, but until then, it's better than nothing," he added.

Chris helped them with the salt lines, and to Brent's surprise, very few people questioned what they were doing.

Maybe they're too weirded out to care at this point.

Once they finished, Brent and Travis set up their laptops at the back table, which Chris had kept open for them.

"We've had enough folks holing up here that we're running a bit thin on some things, so I hope you don't mind grilled cheese sandwiches and chips tonight," he said, putting plates down in front of them.

"Thanks, Chris," Brent replied. "That sounds fantastic. I love grilled cheese."

"How's Liz doing with the shelters?" Travis asked before he took a bite of the hot, gooey sandwich.

"Run ragged," Chris answered. "Like everyone. She wants to commandeer the school buses and evacuate the town, but that's more complicated than you'd think. Takes time to set up places for people to go, especially folks with kids or pets or who need special medical help. I hate to say it, but I think she's right."

"Have you heard from the guy at the dam?" Brent wasn't sure he wanted confirmation of his fears.

"Pete got a call through—the cell signal wasn't good. He says that the dam is holding—for now. But he's trying to release the pressure so it doesn't fail completely. That still means flooding, just maybe not catastrophic."

"Back to the buses—how far would they need to go to be safe?"

Travis pressed. "I run a halfway house in Pittsburgh. I know people who run emergency housing, and maybe some of them have contacts near here. It's worth a shot."

Chris nodded. "Yeah. It is. I'll call Liz." He went straight to voice-mail and left a brief message. "Maybe you can see if any of your contacts can help while we wait for her to reply."

"Let me see who I can get in touch with and what we can manage," Travis offered.

Brent had the awful feeling they were a couple of days too late to make it work.

Chris went back to the bar, taking their empty plates with him.

"We still have an hour before Wyrick's ex-patients show—assuming any of them agree to come," Brent said. "Why don't you see who you can contact about taking in the refugees, and I'll check in with Simon?"

Simon answered on the first ring. "Good timing—I was just going to call. You always have the most interesting world-ending calamities."

"Gee, thanks—I think."

"Okay, here's what I've found so far. Shubin can't be destroyed because they're place spirits. But they can be weakened. I'm emailing you details. It's folklore, so a lot of the instructions contradict each other, but the crux seems to be cleansing the Shubin's lair."

Brent felt his hopes plummet. "It's a mine with hundreds of miles of tunnels. All of it is long abandoned and a death trap. That's going to be tough." He paused. "And the tulpas?"

"According to the lore, tulpas can be 'unmade' just like they can be created," Simon told him. "At least, that's true for regular ones. I don't know what other magics Wyrick might have added to the tulpas he wanted to strengthen and control."

"How do we unmake the tulpas?"

"The people whose fears created them and who willed them into being have to un-will them," Simon replied. "They basically ignore the tulpas out of existence."

"That...could be difficult. We're not sure who all of Wyrick's patients were or if they're still alive and still in town. I'm hoping that at least a few will show up to talk to us." Brent sighed. "We'll come up with something. We always do. Did you see the materials I sent you?"

"Yeah—downloaded them, shared the files with the Alliance, but I've only had a chance to skim part of it," Simon admitted. "Scary as fuck."

"Unfortunately, everything I've read so far from Wyrick's files is about creating these monsters and making them stronger, but he didn't seem to think about how to defuse them after the war."

"His type never do," Simon said. "That's why there are thousands of land mines and unexploded bombs in old war zones all over the world."

Brent's phone buzzed, reminding him that Wyrick's former patients should be arriving soon. "Gotta go. Thank you for everything, and if you get a breakthrough—"

"I'll call. Be careful. Do your best to get out of there in one piece."

"That's the plan." Brent hung up but didn't add that he had started to wonder if any of them would make it out of South Fork alive. He looked up and caught Travis's eye. "Any luck?"

Travis made a see-sawing gesture. "I found some connections and asked for help. Problem is, South Fork isn't the only place in danger of flooding. There's a storm front hanging over a large stretch of Central PA, and shelters are filling up with local folks who don't have anywhere to go."

"Spending a night on a bus in a truck stop parking lot beats drowning."

"Yes—and if it comes down to that, we'll deal. But it would be better if we didn't have to." Travis drummed his fingers on the table. "I'm hoping some of my other contacts will come through."

Brent's watch vibrated again, marking six o'clock. Right on time, the door opened, sending a gust of wind into the room as a dark-haired man in biker leathers entered. A blond man wearing a polo shirt and khaki pants rose from his seat at the bar. Both nodded in greeting as if neither were surprised to see the other.

"You wanted to talk about Dr. Wyrick?" the man who had come from outside asked. "You gonna finally do something about those abominations we helped him create?"

The other man spoke up. "Don't blame yourself, Vinnie. We didn't know what he was doing."

"You don't feel responsible, Jackson? 'Cause I can't sleep at night. I hear them howling. And now with people missing, I think maybe I should go looking for them to see if my Casper would go away if I just let it have me," Vinnie replied.

Travis cleared his throat. "We're hoping you can help us come up with a way to get rid of the creatures without anyone becoming a sacrifice. Please, have a seat and tell us anything you can about your time with Dr. Wyrick."

Vinnie and Jackson exchanged a look, an unspoken contest of wills. It was clear to Brent that while they knew each other and might have shared the experience of combat, the men weren't friends. Brent replaced the salt line at the door, and returned to take his seat.

"I'll go first," Vinnie growled. "I came back from the war fucked in the head." He glared as if daring them to argue.

"I served in Iraq," Brent said. "I understand."

Vinnie seemed to take his measure and then nodded. "Then you know. You see things over there. It messes you up. I wasn't dealing well. Too much booze, too many fights, wife left me, lost my job. Judge sent me to 'court-mandated therapy,' and I got Wyrick. Lucky me."

Despite his gruff manner, Vinnie's leg jiggled, and he twisted a paper napkin as he spoke. "I didn't like him, but it was talk to the shrink or do time. Wyrick was creepy. He was one of those guys who pretends to be your best friend, but really he's looking for dirt he can use on you—know what I mean?"

"I'm not sure I do," Travis replied.

"Wyrick was all touchy-feely, super-compassionate, but it never seemed real," Vinnie said. "At least, I didn't think so. He kept wanting me to picture what I feared the most and pour all my anger and fear into that image. Wyrick said if we transferred our emotions to the thing we imagined, it would lessen the pain. He lied."

"Did he teach you to make thought forms?" Brent asked. "Basically, an invisible friend?"

Vinnie laughed, a harsh, bitter sound. "Yeah. Caspers. I told him it was fuckin' insulting, but he wasn't shy about holding jail over my head. I tried. I mean, I've got a lot of anger to spare. I guess I shouldn't be surprised that it worked. Except what I created was spooky as shit."

"You saw something?" Brent gripped his coffee cup and leaned forward.

Vinnie grimaced. "I'm still not sure exactly *what* I saw, but I can tell you what I *think* I saw. I had a lot of anger going into the Army and even more coming out. I thought it was going to tear me apart from the inside or get me killed in a bar brawl. Wyrick told me to picture how I felt—so I thought of the old movies I used to watch, and I pictured the Wolfman."

"What happened?" Travis glanced at Brent, who knew his partner was thinking about the creature that had jumped on their car.

"For a while, nothing. Every session, doc made me picture the wolfman—how he sounded, what his fur felt like, how he smelled. It got easier to do, putting an image together in my mind," Vinnie went on. "Then our appointments changed, and Doc wanted me to meditate and imagine having a conversation with the wolf and feeding it my anger like meat."

Vinnie shrugged. "I thought it was a bunch of bullshit. Went along with it to stay out of jail. But then..." He turned and stared toward the rain-lashed window, and Brent thought he glimpsed fear behind the tough exterior.

"...weird things started to happen. I'd catch a glimpse of the wolfman during the day when I wasn't even thinking about therapy.

At night, I heard something scratching outside my house, and there were claw marks on the wood by the bedroom window," Vinnie continued. "I'd hear howling, and if I looked out my window, I'd see a dark shape, like the wolf. After that happened a few times, I just put my pillow over my head and stayed in bed."

"Did the wolfman ever attack you?" Brent asked.

Vinnie stared at him for a moment as if trying to figure out whether he was being mocked. Finally, he shook his head.

"No. But even though I was going to my sessions, I still had a lot of rage inside. One night I got in a bar fight, and we both knocked each other around pretty hard. Blowing off steam, not trying to kill anyone. That's when I saw the wolf in the shadows. He had red eyes, and I could see his teeth. And I just knew in my bones that if I called him, he'd tear the other guy apart," Vinnie replied.

"What happened?" Brent felt a chill at Vinnie's story.

"I told the guy it was over and to go back inside. And I thought real hard at the wolf to go away. He did—that night."

"And since then?" Travis prodded.

"Not too long afterward, Wyrick 'fell' out of his window." Vinnie's tone made it clear he didn't believe the official story. "They ended the program, and I got my walking papers. I stopped concentrating on the wolf, and whenever I thought of him or got a glimpse of something in the shadows, I told him to go away. But he doesn't listen to me anymore."

"Did Wyrick give you any special medicines or have any unusual rituals you were supposed to do to create the shadow creature?" Travis had a look in his eye that usually meant he'd found a clue.

"No. They drug tested us all the time, so I'd have known. Rituals? You mean like witchy stuff? Nah. Although the doc always said the same thing when we started picturing the wolf—said it was supposed to open my mind to free my rage," Vinnie told them.

"Do you remember what he said?" Brent tried not to sound too excited.

Vinnie shifted in his chair. "I'd, um, rather not say it out loud. I can write it down for you." He glanced back at the window. "He's out there—my wolfman. I don't want him to get any closer."

"Did you ever see any other creatures aside from the one you imagined?" Travis asked. Jackson shook his head, but Vinnie caught his breath and looked away.

"Vinnie?" Travis asked gently.

"The old man," Vinnie said quietly. "I've never told anyone—not even Wyrick. But all my life, just before something bad happened, I'd see this old man in a fur coat in my dreams. I don't think he's anyone I've ever met. Always scared the shit out of me. Even as a kid, I knew he was bad. I saw him on and off during the war, right before a clusterfuck. Lately, it's been more often. Sleeping pills don't work, but if I get drunk enough, I can sometimes get a few hours rest before he shows up again."

Brent took a good look at Vinnie and could see the toll his "bad dreams" had taken.

Brent pulled a piece of paper from a tablet in his bag and slid it and a pen over to Vinnie. "Thank you for talking with us." He suspected that it had been hard for Vinnie to share his concerns.

"What are you going to do about it?" Vinnie demanded after he scribbled the remembered words and passed the paper and pen back to Brent. "Those things all of us made are still around, and they've gotten worse. They used to chase people or scare them, not kill. Don't know what changed things. Now, ain't none of us going to be safe until they're gone."

"He's right," Jackson spoke up. "That's what happened to me with Wyrick, except they held my job over my head, not jail. I made a cat creature, not a wolfman, but the rest is the same." He paused. "I remember the 'relaxation words' too—if you want me to write them down for you."

Brent thought about Vinnie's "wolfman" and Jackson's mention of a were-cat. *So that's what we saw. Tulpas they created and Wyrick strengthened into something that's still around.*

Brent gave him paper and pen, and Jackson wrote quickly.

Clearly the "meditation" introduction had stuck in his memory. While they waited, Chris brought coffee for them and Brent thanked him with a nod.

"And you think your...creature...is still out there too?" Travis asked Jackson.

He nodded. "I know he is. I see him—more often these last few weeks than before. And when I think at him to go away, he just stares at me, like he's gloating. I can't control him anymore—if I ever really could," Jackson admitted.

Brent turned back to Vinnie. "You don't seem to buy the story that Dr. Wyrick's death was an accident. Why?"

Vinnie and Jackson shared another glance, an unspoken conversation between men who might not be friends but had been through hell together.

"Nobody liked Dr. Wyrick. He was an arrogant son of a bitch, and he lorded his power over people. For us, it was that he could throw us back in jail or get us in trouble if we didn't do what he said. But he bullied the hospital people too, about how he'd bring the feds down on them if he didn't get his way." Vinnie shrugged.

"He was too full of himself to jump," Jackson put in. "His kind always think they've got it all figured out. Lots of people didn't like him, but I always wondered if the feds didn't give him a shove."

Travis raised an eyebrow. "Interesting theory. Why?"

Jackson hesitated for a moment as if worried that he'd said too much before barreling on. "They'd show up every couple of weeks, and it didn't seem like he got along with them. Once, I heard them shouting when I came early for my appointment. I didn't hear what they said, but no one was happy."

"I heard him say something on the phone about 'taking what he'd developed and going solo,'" Vinnie chimed in. "He ended the call as soon as he realized I was there and looked like he'd sucked on a dill pickle when he figured out that I'd heard him talking. He didn't say anything, and neither did I. But maybe the feds didn't want him to leave."

That summed up Brent's suspicions, and he felt certain Travis shared those same thoughts.

"Thank you for talking with us," Brent said. "I know the military doesn't make it easy to talk about this stuff."

Vinnie shook his head, looking a bit lost. "When I started my sessions with Wyrick, a little part of me hoped he could help me get rid of the anger so I wouldn't become a monster. And because of him, I've created an even worse thing and put it out into the world."

To Brent's surprise, Jackson reached out and laid a hand on Vinnie's arm. "We got screwed—by the V.A. and by Wyrick. That's not on you or me. Out of everything we've done, this isn't something we did wrong."

Vinnie managed a tight smile and a brusque nod of his head. His gaze snapped up to bore into Brent. "If there's a way to kill these shadows, you tell us, hear me? I need a chance to put this right."

"If there's a way you can help, I'll make sure you know," Brent promised.

Vinnie and Jackson rose, and Brent and Travis also stood. Just as Vinnie took a step toward the door, a loud *boom* shook the tavern, rattling the bottles on the backbar and the glass in the windows.

"Holy shit!" One of the customers seated near the front window stared and pointed.

An orange fireball rose into the sky. Everyone rushed to see. Chris paled, reaching beneath the bar for a police scanner and placing it on the counter. He turned up the volume.

"...all units to the East Conemaugh Bridge, South Fork side. Do not attempt to cross. Truck explosion in the center of the span, structure is compromised." Calabrese's voice sounded worried and dead tired.

"Fuck," Chris muttered, scrabbling for his phone. He hit speed dial, and Brent heard it ring until Liz's voicemail picked up.

"What's going on?" Brent sidled up to the bar even as the others remained glued to the window, watching the distant flames.

"Liz got a bus and a driver lined up—they were going to take the first bunch of...refugees...to Johnstown," Chris said. "She found a church that will put them up for at least a couple of nights. They were just leaving—"

Brent saw the fear in his old friend's eyes. "That doesn't mean the bus was on the bridge when it blew."

"Can't prove she wasn't," Chris said in a voice like he'd gargled glass.

"Save the grieving until you know for sure," Brent said, dropping his voice to a near whisper.

Chris's phone rang, and he grabbed for it like a drowning man. "Liz? My God, are you okay? Where are you?"

Liz spoke too fast for Brent to pick up on the conversation, except for what mattered—she was alive.

"Okay, okay. Just—be safe. Text me and let me know how things are going. If you need provisions, I'm running thin, but I'll give you whatever I can." He listened for a moment and nodded. "Yeah. Love you too."

Chris ended the call and stared at the phone for a moment. "She's alive," he said, and Brent wondered if it was more to reassure himself than to inform them. "They loaded the bus and were heading out, but everything took longer, and so they were behind schedule. She said a big truck passed them, and then they were about a block away when the explosion happened. She thinks it was that truck."

"They're safe. Liz is okay. Breathe," Brent coaxed.

Chris nodded. "I know. It's just going to take a bit to sink in."

The police radio squawked again as the bar's customers slowly returned to their seats.

"Mike, report," Calabrese ordered on the police channel.

"Negative on the West River Bridge," Sokolowki replied, sounding disgusted. "The water is high and rough. It's compromised at least one of the supports. I'll be surprised if it's still standing by tomorrow night."

"How are the northern roads?" Calabrese asked.

"They're a clusterfuck," Mike replied, sounding too frustrated to worry about protocol. "A sinkhole took out both lanes on River Road in the valley, and mud and rockslides completely blocked Hillside at the cut. No one's getting out that way."

"Talk to us," Travis said. "What does that mean?"

Chris poured himself a shot of Jack and knocked it back. "There are four ways in or out of South Fork—the bridges and two main roads. The bridges are out. And apparently, so are both of the roads."

Just like what Darius warned us about at the diner. Darkness and hell on the other side of the bridge into South Fork.

"Can't people just go around the blockage?" Brent asked, trying to recall the map he'd studied on their way to town.

Chris shook his head. "Not with where the problems are. There's a natural bottleneck on each road—a valley and a cut through the mountain. No matter how you get to the roads, you've got to pass through those bottlenecks to make it to the other side—short of hiking over Lee Mountain."

"Can it be done? The hike?" Travis pressed.

"Sure—on a nice day when it hasn't been raining for a week if you're a mid-level or better hiker," Chris said. "I've done it—in a dry summer when I was in good shape, and it still took a lot out of me."

He gestured in the general direction of the roads. "Now? It's a death trap. Even if most of the people in town weren't older and not athletic, all this rain is going to have washed out trails, and it's prime for mudslides and rock falls. No chance we're getting people out that way."

Chris fixed them both with his gaze. "You get what this means? We're trapped in town with those monsters, and if they don't kill us, the flood when the dam breaks will wipe South Fork off the map. If you've got a solution, you'd better pull it out of your asses, or we're all going to die."

CHAPTER NINE

"WE'VE BEEN in town less than three days, and it's go-time," Travis said once he and Brent returned to their table with a fresh pot of hot coffee.

"These things never come with an instruction manual," Brent agreed.

Travis's phone rang, and he felt a surge of relief to recognize Simon Kincaide's ringtone. "I'm hoping you've got answers because it's getting rough over here," he said.

"It's lore. That means I've got opinions, few of which agree with each other," Simon replied. "I also tapped into our network, so I have input from several witches, a necromancer, psychics, and a couple of other mediums."

Travis trusted Simon's skills as a psychic medium, and knew that his friends were equally reliable and powerful in their own gifts. A few might even be immortal. "I'll take anything you've got," he told Simon as Brent leaned in to listen.

"I found a ritual to dispel 'conjured spirits,'" Simon went on. "That phrase can have several meanings, but it usually carries the sense of a witch summoning the spirit from somewhere or perhaps creating them from elemental materials. Which is pretty close to creating a thought form out of will and imagination."

"Close—but is it close enough?" Travis asked. Magic could be as nitpicky as the most legalistic lawyer, and he didn't want to risk all their lives on a "maybe."

"The witches I bounced the idea around with all thought so—and they've got more than a few lifetimes of magical experience among them," Simon replied. "It's a combination of a cleansing, banishment, and exorcism, with the goal being to obliterate the spirits completely, not just send them back to wherever they came from."

"Give me the gist of it," Travis said. "It better be simple—we're a long way from the nearest botanica to get supplies."

"Fortunately, you can raid the kitchen for what you need. Salt, sage, rue, dill, rosemary, and thyme repel spirits—and the grocery store spice rack varieties will work just fine in a pinch. Combine those in a cup—best if the cup is silver, but anything will do. "Salt water cleanses, so if there's any way to hose the haunted area down with some, it will help to weaken the tulpas," Simon suggested.

Brent elbowed Travis. "Would road salt and rainwater do?"

"They should. Then cut juniper branches—boxwood if you can get it—and make a fire," Simon advised.

"Here's the tricky part—get the people who have seen or created the tulpas to draw the monsters. Everyone who fears them also contributes energy to sustain the thought forms. The more pictures, the better. Burn the pictures on the juniper-boxwood fire, and pour the powdered plant mixture over it while you say the cleansing/banishment/exorcism. The more people who believe what you're doing will destroy the tulpas, the better because these are thought creatures," Simon warned.

"Fuck," Travis murmured. "Tammy's art project at the library."

Brent nodded. "Wyrick had his patients do the same thing. I wonder if he meant to create a failsafe in case the tulpas got too much to handle."

"It explains why the fire and salt rounds made them vanish but didn't keep them away for good," Travis said.

"I'll email you the litany," Simon told them. "Tweak it as the power speaks to you. But it should have the essential elements."

"Thank you. What about the Shubin?"

"Yeah, he's more of a challenge because he's not conjured. Odds are good he's some sort of twisted elemental energy, so he can be weakened and bound, but not destroyed," Simon replied. "They're hard to get rid of because they like the deep places—if not mines, then caves—that people can't access. Salt, iron, and holy water weaken them. There's also a rather obscure text I found that uses a proxy for a binding ritual."

Simon paused. "The proxy is a carved figure made from coal. Cannel coal, if you can find it, which has been associated with protective magic for a long time. In mining regions, 'Cannelmancy' was a folk magic usually worked by women to appease the deep spirits and keep the miners safe. You don't hear much about it these days, but it might be something you can use. I'll keep digging, but that's all I've got right now. Sorry."

"No reason to apologize—it's more than we had before," Travis assured him. "It's getting dicey here—if we get cut off, you'll know we lost signal. Light a candle for us—we're going to need it."

The call ended, and Travis slipped his phone into his pocket. Brent fiddled with his coffee cup, and Travis could tell that something was bothering his partner.

"What's on your mind? I mean, besides the end of the world —again."

That raised a rueful chuckle from Brent. "I've just been thinking, with all this talk about tulpas—is that what Danny is? Did I somehow 'make' his ghost because I missed him so much?"

Travis felt a cold breeze, and the salt shaker abruptly fell over. Brent glared at the fallen shaker. "That doesn't prove anything, for or against. Tulpas can affect physical things, just like ghosts."

The glass shaker rolled back and forth. "Don't spill salt," Brent said. "It's bad luck."

Travis could sense Danny's spirit, weaker than it had been before Cooper City but growing stronger. "Relax. Danny's a ghost, not a tulpa. I can see him, and the energy is different from the tulpas."

"You're sure?"

Travis nodded, and the salt shaker righted itself, untouched. "Positive."

Brent grinned, elated at the news. "I'm glad. It's good to have him back." He closed his eyes, and his smile faded as he realized the danger.

Please, Danny. Don't risk it. You're just coming back. Let us handle it, he thought to the ghost.

Travis still felt Danny's presence, but he could not hear the mental conversation.

"What's wrong?" Travis nudged, worried by the one-sided argument he could hear.

Brent opened his eyes. "Danny wants to help. He isn't as strong as he was before Cooper City, but he wants to rally the miners' ghosts to hold off the tulpas. I don't know if they could hurt him. He's only now come back. I can't lose him again."

Travis shut his eyes and opened himself up to his gift, not just sending spirits but channeling them as a true medium. He felt Danny's spirit inhabit him and withdrew his own consciousness to a corner of his mind where he could observe, but not interfere.

"Brent. Let me help." Travis's voice changed, no longer his usual speaking tone, and Brent's head snapped up, catching something familiar.

"Danny?"

Travis nodded, channeling Danny. "I can't stay long. Your friend will need his strength for other things. But I need to help."

"I've missed you so much," Brent said, blinking back tears as his voice grew hoarse. "Don't ask me to deal with you vanishing again."

Danny/Travis chuckled sadly. "I fought my way back to you, and

I don't intend to leave. But I also don't want to see you on this side any time soon. So let me protect you. Protection goes both ways. It's what brothers do," Danny's ghost reminded his twin.

Brent clenched his jaw, and it looked to Travis as if his partner fought a silent internal war. Finally, he nodded.

"Okay. I get that. But don't go sacrificing yourself again. Once was enough."

Travis felt Danny's emotions, a flood of sadness, love, and fond exasperation. "I'm already dead. If the grief demons didn't destroy me, those mangy shadow dogs aren't going to."

"You don't know that."

"I do know that they can kill you—and Travis too," Danny argued, and Travis knew that while Brent could be reckless about his own safety, he was almost as protective of Travis as he was of Danny.

"That's cheating," Brent countered.

Danny/Travis shrugged. "Whatever it takes. Do we have a deal? I need to let him go."

"Okay," Brent replied grudgingly. "But—be careful, and don't do anything stupid."

"Who, me? That's my older brother's job," Danny jibed, joking about the minutes-difference between their ages. "I'll see you after."

The ghost disentangled himself from Travis's consciousness, leaving him breathless. He reached for his coffee, dumped in more sugar, and knocked it back.

"Travis? Is he gone?"

Travis nodded, but he waited another minute before he looked directly at Brent, giving his partner a chance to compose himself. "Yeah, it's me again. Danny was telling the truth. I don't think the tulpas can hurt the ghosts, but the spirits running interference for us could help a lot. He missed you as much as you missed him," Travis added, knowing how bereft Brent had been during the months when he feared Danny's ghost might be gone forever.

"Yeah, yeah. He was always the sappy one," Brent grumbled, voice rough. "Thank you for doing that. I know it takes a lot out of you." Despite his worry, he couldn't hide his relief and joy at Danny's return.

Travis took a deep breath, monitoring himself as he had learned to do when working spells or using his abilities. "He wasn't difficult to channel, and he didn't overstay his welcome. I'm fine." *Which is good because we've got a long night ahead of us.*

"Did you think about what Vinnie and Jackson told us?" Brent asked.

Travis paused for a sip of coffee. "I think they're probably right about Wyrick. As for the 'meditation' he had them use—it's standard stuff. Nothing magical about it, although by taking them into a hypnotic state, he lowered their mental barriers. That would make it easier to feed energy into creating the tulpas."

The police scanner shrilled, silencing the conversations in the bar. "We need flashers and sawhorses on Mead Road near the miner monument," Calabrese's voice crackled across the connection. "Got a new sinkhole. Stay well back from the edge—it's probably going to get bigger."

"Didn't Tammy tell us that the mines went under the memorial?" Brent asked.

"Yeah. She said they basically were underneath the whole town."

"Let's see if Mike can commandeer a salt truck to spread on the roads and slow the tulpas down while we work the ritual to get rid of them."

"Dumping a load of salt down the sinkhole probably wouldn't be a bad idea either," Travis mused. "Especially with the amount of water that'll be going down with it."

The lights in the bar flickered wildly, and Brent shot a look at Travis, who shook his head.

"Not ghosts," Travis said.

In the next moment, the bar plunged into darkness.

"Everyone stay where you are," Chris's voice rang out. "I'm going to get the generator fired up. It'll just be a minute."

They heard his footsteps head for the kitchen, and then the

crowded room fell silent. Without the hum of voices, Travis could hear the rain beating on the roof and windows, steady and hard. It felt as if the patrons held their breath until the generator chugged to life and the lights came back on, dimmed but glowing.

The door swung open, and Nonna stomped inside, rain streaming from her black trench coat and umbrella. Tammy followed a few steps behind, bedraggled and apologetic.

"I need to talk to you." Nonna furled her umbrella and pointed it like a wand at Travis and Brent in the back corner.

"There was no talking her out of coming, no matter what the storm was doing," Tammy said to the room at large.

Brent and Travis rose as she approached, and Brent offered Nonna a chair. She sat, but Tammy stayed standing, out of the way.

"Figured you might need these—there's power in them," Nonna said, putting a soggy cardboard box on the table. Travis wiped off the rain and peeked inside to see a stack of hand-drawn pictures.

"Brought you these too." Nonna withdrew a container of black dust from the large carpetbag she carried and a figure carved from coal of an old man in a bulky coat with a big hat. Travis wondered if it was the piece she had been carving at the library.

"You ever heard of cannelmancy?" Nonna asked.

Travis's eyes narrowed. "Yes, but I don't know much."

Nonna's thin lips twitched with a pleased smile. "Cannel coal is special—a perfect conduit for power. My family came from a coal mining area in Italy. The magic follows our line. Our men go below, and our women work spells and pray to the old gods to bring them back into the light once more."

"If you can do coal magic—cannelmancy—begging your pardon, why are the shadow creatures still here?" Brent asked.

Nonna reared back and then sighed. "I lost my nerve. Ten years ago after a cave-in I tried to use my magic to save the trapped miners. It wasn't enough. They died. After that, I told myself folks were better off without my meddling. But now, things are bad enough that I can't make it worse. So, I'm here to help."

"Thank you." Travis appreciated the old witch's candor. "We need all the allies we can get."

Nonna withdrew an envelope and slid it across the table. "I've been working on a spell for a while, hoping I'd never have to use it. But even though I was running away from my failure, I could see what was happening. The shadows in the dark, the people going missing, and the Shubin—"

"You know about Shubin?" Travis interrupted.

Nonna rolled her eyes. "My people were miners and mine witches. We knew the Shubin were terrible enemies and treacherous allies. We sacrificed to them and made offerings. And we made sure they understood that if necessary, we could bind them."

Travis reached for the envelope. "And you know how to bind them?"

"I have my great-grandmother's spell book. Her description of how it was done in her day. The last time, as far as I know, that anyone made it happen," Nonna said.

"Can you do it?" Brent looked from the envelope to the old woman.

"Not alone. My coven sisters are dead or too frail to attempt the working." Nonna looked to Travis. "But you have real power. The ghosts listen to you—and they are reliable allies. There are two more who have abilities we could draw to our team—if they have the courage to try."

"Father Prochazka," Travis said.

"And Krystyk," Brent added, looking surprised as if the idea had just occurred to him.

Nonna nodded. "Yes. They have small magics, but still real."

"Like my Night Vigil," Travis murmured.

"How do we reach them?" Brent held up his phone. "There's no signal. The towers must be down."

"They will come," Nonna said with an enigmatic smile.

Travis leaned over to his keyboard and logged in, then looked up. "Internet's out. We're on our own."

Brent looked to Tammy. "You told us about an old railroad tunnel. Can we get people to safety that way if the roads and bridges are down? It hasn't stopped raining. The rivers will rise higher—and if the dam gives way, nowhere in the valley is safe."

"Tony and I talked about the tunnel," she replied. "There's no telling what's in there—the sneaks like the dark. But assuming there aren't monsters, it's a hike up a steep, unfinished road and a dirt trail through the tunnel. School buses won't make it, and most of the people in the shelters can't climb."

"We can't stop the rain or fix the dam," Travis said. "Let's focus on the Shubin and the tulpas—if we get them out of the way, moving people to safety will be less likely to get us all killed."

"I don't know if this helps, but my friend Aimee's been teaching free yoga and meditation classes to the people holed up in the library," Tammy piped up. "Tonight, she's having people imagine their fears about the sneaks—and then picture them blowing away on the wind."

"I might have suggested that," Nonna said. "If imagination and will can create a creature, it can unmake them as well."

"That helps a lot," Travis told Tammy. "Having people dispel their fear and picture disintegrating the tulpas really can make a difference." He noticed the large, police-grade walkie-talkie clipped to Tammy's belt. "Can you reach the folks at the library with that?"

"Should be able to."

"I've got an addition to your 'positive thinking' exercise at the library, but the timing matters," Travis said. "When we get ready to banish the tulpas, having as many people as possible chant their disbelief in unison might carry some power to send them away."

Brent gave him a bemused look. "Like 'tulpa, tulpa, go away, don't come back another day'?"

"Oh, how about 'hell no, tulpas go!'" Tammy suggested, then grimaced. "Forget that—we can't have the kids swearing."

"I was thinking more along the lines of 'tulpas leave—we don't believe,'" Travis said. "Short, to the point, and it rhymes. Maybe if you explain what we're doing, Chris can lead the bar in a couple of rounds too." He checked his watch. "Give us half an hour, and have everyone start chanting at ten."

"That would work," Tammy said. "Liz has a walkie-talkie too. She'll be up for it—and there are a lot of older people at both our centers, so you might get some of the original veterans who were involved in Wyrick's program."

"You and Liz are awesome," Travis said.

Outside, the wind howled, rain rattled against the windows and pelted the roof, and the low drone of the police radio announced one catastrophe after another.

Cars swept away by floodwaters damaged everything in their wake.

Roofs collapsed from the weight of the rainwater, and gas-powered machinery stalled and malfunctioned in the downpour.

Names of people were reported missing and their last known location as well as warnings about shadow creatures.

The radio kept up its litany, convincing Travis that they had run out of time.

"Let's start with the tulpas," Travis said. "We need juniper branches to make a fire."

"Juniper? There's a bunch out behind the building. Gonna be soaked, but if you pat them dry, gasoline should do just fine," Chris told them. He looked at the men at the bar. "Get off your asses and help them cut branches, or turn your truck lights on so they can see."

"Do we get a free beer?" one of the men asked.

Chris cuffed him on the side of the head. "No, but we might have a town left in the morning. Now, git!"

Half a dozen men scrambled to do the bartender's bidding. Tammy walked over to the bar to explain the chant idea to Chris. Brent shot his friend a salute in thanks and went outside to help.

Two guys angled their trucks so the headlights provided enough light to see. Brent and Travis had their shotguns, and another man got his rifle from the rack in the back of his pickup to stand guard while they cut juniper branches.

In the darkness beyond the reach of the headlights, Travis heard footfalls and low growls. Now and again, the lights caught a red or gold reflection from the shadows, or the flash of white teeth.

"It's pretty wet out here," one of the barflies observed. "Gonna be hard to make a bonfire."

"How about the picnic shelter?" Another man said, pointing to the open-air enclosure. The tables had been stacked for the off-season, leaving most of the asphalt floor empty. Travis didn't think the fire would endanger the roof, but if it did, that seemed a small price to pay to get rid of the tulpas.

"Let's do it," Travis said.

Brent and the man with the hunting rifle stood guard as they hauled the juniper branches into the enclosure. Travis rounded up enough rags to dry most of the water from the boughs and stack them for a fire.

"I've got a can of gas in my truck. Might be the only way you'll get those to burn since they're still damp," one of the men said.

"I'll cover you," Brent volunteered. They walked into the head-lights and between the vehicles to get to a pickup that sat a few feet farther back in the shadows.

A screech like a mountain lion split the night, and then two shotgun blasts, a yowl of pain, and a lot of cursing. Travis handed off his shotgun to one of the barflies, who ran toward the noise.

Minutes later, the four men emerged from the shadows. The gas can man leaned heavily on Brent, and he had a gash in his leg.

"Here's your gas." Brent handed off the container. "Got jumped by that damn were-cat we saw—or one just like it. He got clawed, but it's not deep." He knelt beside the injured man and ripped strips off of his shirt to bandage the injury. "I'd rather not risk trying to get back across the lot to the bar until we're done here."

Travis had already laid a salt circle inside the shelter and set up the ritual ingredients in a stainless steel mixing bowl—the closest thing Chris had to a silver chalice. The darkness at the edges of the parking lot thrummed with unnatural energy. Travis sensed the tulpas, who prowled like hungry predators, eyeing their warm bodies for a next meal.

"If something in the shadows comes at you, swing like you're in the World Series." Brent handed out lengths of rebar and then picked up his shotgun. "I've got rock salt rounds. Iron and salt should keep the shadow creatures at bay. We can't let them through to disrupt the ritual. They've killed enough people—we need to stop them."

The men looked terrified, but to their credit, they stood their ground.

A low growl came from the shadows, echoed by more of the monsters lurking just out of sight. The men took a half step closer to the center of the enclosure, a primal response from a hindbrain that still remembered sharp teeth in the dark.

Some of the creatures looked like large hellhounds—the movie version, not the real beasts Travis and Brent had fought more than once. Then again, if the tulpas were fashioned from people's fears, those images would be fueled by Hollywood special effects.

One of the tulpas was a big cat, and Travis wondered if it was the one they had fought at the lumberyard. A bristle-haired monster with elongated limbs and a misshapen head lurked at the edge of the light, and Travis guessed it was Vinnie's wolfman.

A huge paw swiped at one of the men who stood too close to the edge of the enclosure, gashing open his shoulder. Brent fired his shotgun, and the tulpa yelped, falling back to pace at the edge of the trees. Another man rushed forward to pull his downed comrade into the center of the circle and bandage his arm.

"Stay inside the salt line," Brent warned, seeing someone else venture close to the edge. Before the man could react, claws swiped at his leg, knocking his feet out from under him and dragging him away.

Brent and the man with Travis's gun fired at the creature while the rifleman used his night scope to squeeze off several rounds at the retreating tulpa. The rifleman moved to go after it, but Brent clamped a hand on his shoulder.

"You won't catch it. He's gone. We need you here." Brent turned back toward the ritual space. "Let's get this done."

The surviving barflies didn't need reminding to stay away from the edge.

"Are you a witch?" One of the men asked Travis.

"No, but I am." Nonna strode across the rain-slick parking lot back-lit by lightning like one of the old gods.

Travis feared the tulpas might attack her, but even they seemed to know better.

"Move out of the way, sonny," she said to one of the barflies who stood in her path, and the man scrambled to make room.

Travis remembered Tammy saying that townsfolk believed Nonna could put the Evil Eye on people. The men from the bar looked at her with a mix of respect and fear.

"The creatures are real because we've believed them into existence," Brent continued. "They take power from what we're afraid of. When we start the ritual, I'm going to need you to do your best to unbelieve them."

"Did you add some coal dust to your mix?" Nonna asked Travis. "It'll carry the spark of my magic along with the power of the spell."

Travis nodded. "I added it right after you gave it to me. Are you ready?"

She gave him a crooked grin that suggested she was relishing the adventure. "Damn straight. Let's send these shadows packing."

A gust of cold wind told Travis that Danny had marshaled help. Ghostly images flickered around the perimeter, outside the salt line but between the living men and the tulpas. Travis reached out to the spirits, strengthening them with as much energy as he could spare.

We can use all the help you can provide, he told the ghosts. *Help us hold off the tulpas so we can end the damage Wyrick caused.*

We're on it, Danny's spirit responded, more solid than he had been since he disappeared in Cooper City. *Keep my brother safe.*

The ghosts grew more solid and spread out to surround the ritual area, taking their role as guardians seriously. Tulpas growled, and Travis could hear the click of their claws against the road as they circled, looking for an advantage.

Brent lit the gas-soaked branches, sending flames high into the air, dancing as the wind gusted. Travis sprinkled the mix of protective plants and then added the drawings from Wyrick's patients and the library refugees, then stepped back as he and Nonna spoke the banishing ritual together.

The smell of juniper hung heavy in the smoky air, and heat made their wet clothing steam in the cold.

Brent checked his watch. "It's ten; they'll be starting to chant." He looked to the cold, frightened men. "Our part is easy. Pretend you're at a football game. Tulpas leave—we don't believe. Tulpas leave, we don't believe..."

Nonna began the spell. Parts of the phrasing were familiar to Travis, who wished he'd had more time to study Simon's notes. The litany drew from the Latin Rite of Exorcism and the even older Banishment Ritual, which he knew well. Other parts were new to him, and he wondered if Nonna had blended them from ancient traditions of the Mediterranean *stregas*.

"Infernal spirits, raised of will and malice, creatures of pain and fear—you have no power here," Travis's voice rang out in Latin above the hiss and pop of the flames.

Nonna spoke in Italian, but Travis remembered the translation from Simon's email. "Be gone, foul spirits. You are no longer needed. Those who called to you are no more. You are released. Go, and do not return."

Outside the salt ring, the firelight added definition to the tulpas' shapes, a shadow menagerie of wolves, hellhounds, big cats, and large, fast reptiles, as well as the wolfman that had ripped up his car. The ghosts blinked in and out, translucent and then nearly solid, fighting the tulpas—fierce protectors beyond the reach of the shadow creatures' teeth and claws. Every second they kept the tulpas at bay bought Travis and Nonna the time they needed to complete the spells.

"Get thee hence," Travis shouted into the wind. "Leave this realm. From nothing you were created, and to nothing you return."

"Let it be so," Nonna responded.

"We don't believe...we don't believe...we don't believe..." Brent and the others chanted, and while he couldn't hear the people inside Fisher's or at the library or community center, Travis knew that their energy lent power to the banishment.

The juniper branch bonfire collapsed, sending blood-red flames high into the air in a constellation of embers. The heat flared, and sweat poured in rivulets down Travis's back despite the cold night. Nonna's flushed face had taken on an ecstatic expression as the power of the ritual called to her magic.

The sharp pine scent filled Travis's nostrils. He could taste it in the back of his throat, along with ash and salt. He blinked hard, trying to clear the smoke from his eyes. A howl like the coming of the Wild Hunt echoed in the night, filled with pain and hunger. The tulpas hurled themselves at the barrier of ghosts and salt one final time, and then their shadow figures broke apart, rising like ash and embers in a spectral whirlwind before vanishing into the night.

As quickly as it rose, the fire died back to orange embers. Beyond the salt circle, the ghosts stilled, an undead honor guard.

"Do you think the monsters are all gone?" one of the men from the bar asked, gripping his rebar white-knuckled.

"One way to find out," Travis replied.

Danny? What's it look like out there?

The monsters disappeared—at least, there aren't any near here.

You did a helluva great job.

Just protecting my stubborn big brother, Danny replied. *And other duties as required.*

Please thank the others for their help. I don't know if the tulpas could hurt spirits, but you saved our asses—and helped save South Fork.

Keep an eye on Brent. He needs a wingman. I'll do my best to be around, but if I can't—

I'll watch his back, Travis promised. *Go get some rest.*

Travis realized that he hadn't responded to the man's question. "Yes. From here at least. I don't know if we sent all of the tulpas packing, but we've plowed the road. It's a good start."

Nonna nodded. "This was the easy part. But now, the way's cleared for us to deal with the Shubin. The night's still young."

Travis's watch vibrated, silently marking the hour. Nine o'clock. "Magic rises at noon—and midnight," he murmured.

"Then we'd best finish preparing," Nonna replied, looking no worse for the wear, although Travis felt the drain on his energy from their magic. "There's work to do."

CHAPTER TEN

WHEN THEY RETURNED to Fisher's, Chris and the others looked up, worried and expectant.

"Did it work?" Chris asked. "We chanted like the ball was on the one-yard line with ten seconds left in the game. Haven't yelled like that since the last time the Steelers were in the Super Bowl."

Travis nodded. "I think so. All the shadow creatures nearby are gone. Thank you for your help shifting the energy. Sometimes, that can make all the difference."

"That's a good start," Chris said. "Better than what we had before."

"Still have to stop the Big Bad," Brent told him. "That's going to take a little more preparation."

Nonna bellied up to the bar and asked for a shot of Uzo, then knocked it back like a pro and slammed the glass down. "Another."

Chris hurried to comply.

The men who had gone outside to help with the tulpa ritual returned to their barstools, soggy and looking worse for the wear. Chris brought out the first aid kit and patched up the gashes for the two who had been attacked. Everyone raised a glass in memory of

Kevin, who had been dragged away. They all looked like they were in shock.

Being afraid of the supernatural is one thing. Finding out that it's real is another, Brent thought. *Chris is going to be selling a lot of alcohol tonight.*

Brent noticed that a few more people had joined the refugees at Fisher's. Jamie from the hardware store was huddled in conversation with Vinnie and Jackson, the soldiers who had been Wyrick's victims.

Good—that's at least two of the people who helped create the tulpas who were on hand to banish them.

Vinnie looked particularly rattled and haggard, with dark circles under his eyes as if he hadn't slept in days. Brent remembered that the man had confided that he also dreamed of an old man in a fur coat—the Shubin.

Was the Shubin working with the tulpas, predators who share the spoils? Could it feel when we banished them? It's an ancient creature. We're just fodder for it. Could it even conceive of us being a threat?

Brent walked over to Vinnie and Jackson. "Thank you for helping send the tulpas away."

"They're gone, but not the old man." Vinnie twitched as he spoke like he'd been doing shots of Red Bull and espresso. "The old man's been here forever. It won't be over until he's gone."

"That's the next project," Brent assured him, doing his best to sound upbeat. *Can't blame him for tweaking a little if he's still dreaming about a killer mine spirit. Maybe once we banish the Shubin, he'll finally have some peace.* "Hang in there," he told them. "We've got a plan."

Brent joined Travis at the table in the back corner. Travis had ordered a big basket of French fries and sodas for each of them. Jamie came over a few minutes later.

"I thought about what you said with the salt and iron pellets. Tammy told me about the old railroad tunnel. We might not be able to get our folks up and out that way, but if we live through this, we might get some rescue vehicles in."

"What did you have in mind?" Brent admired the way Liz and her friends had stepped up to protect South Fork.

"I loaded up my 4WD truck with all the road salt we had left and every box of iron buckshot, plus a couple of double barrels and some high-lumen jack lights. I'm going to put the folks in here to work packing shells, and then Jackson is going to ride shotgun and blast away while I spread salt and light that tunnel up like the sun."

She smirked. "If there's anything left in there, we're going to send it back to where it came from."

"Give us a bit more time," Travis said. "We need to do another ritual at midnight when the magic is strongest. It won't fix the flooding or the rock slides, but it should bind the malicious mine spirit that's been making everything worse."

Jamie raised an eyebrow. "Do I even want to know?"

Brent shook his head. "Probably not."

Jamie headed back to Jackson. Vinnie had slipped away while she had been gone. Nonna joined Travis and Brent at their table after she downed another shot. The liquor didn't seem to affect her. "Good work with the shadow creatures. The Shubin will be worse—you know that, right?"

Travis nodded. "I suspected as much."

"My cannelmancy will affect the Shubin's essence since he is bound to the coal. Destroying the likeness will weaken him since I've poured magic into the figure to limit his power and tie him to the deep places," Nonna said.

"That alone isn't enough because the Shubin did not become as he is naturally. That son of a bitch Wyrick tampered with powers he didn't understand," Nonna continued, crossing herself and muttering a more colorful insult in Italian. "He made the Shubin more dangerous than he would have normally become, and the shadow creatures' murders fed the dark energy even more."

They looked up as the door opened. Father Prochazka wandered into Fisher's. He ignored the looks others gave him and made his way to the back table.

"I took a walk, and here I am," he told them. "The church is full, lit up with candles. I have nothing to give them—no assurance of salvation in this world or the next, no comfort. I've never felt so useless in my life."

Father Prochazka set a small canvas bag on the table, and then he reached into his jacket pocket and withdrew an old leather book. The binding's finish had flaked, and the title's gold leaf was faded. "My predecessor left this with a letter of instruction for the next priest. He researched a purification ritual, fearing that the darkness in the mines would rise."

"We're glad you're here," Travis told him. "Pull up a chair. We've got some time before midnight, so we've got to make this count."

———

"YOU EXPECT THIS TO WORK?" Calabrese stood hunched against the rain, hands in his pockets. They had left the refuge of the bar and headed into the storm to work the ritual.

"It's a Hail Mary pass, but it's our best shot," Brent admitted.

"No pressure, but the river's already over its banks. The dam hasn't broken—yet. Don't know how long that will last. Pete managed to get another call through—the dam's overflow valves aren't working right, so he's got to adjust them by hand. He's trying to reduce the pressure to keep the breastworks from failing. It's not looking good. If you can do anything to better our odds, I'm all for it," the sheriff told him.

"You've already done a lot," Brent replied, looking at what Calabrese had pulled together as the clock ticked toward midnight.

Mike Sokolowski sat at the wheel of a huge dump truck loaded with road salt. Eight public works trucks ringed the area around the largest sinkhole, lighting up the rainy night with their powerful headlights.

Rainwater poured over the ragged rim of the hole, falling deep into the abandoned mine. The Miner Memorial's granite cast a long shadow as if the dead knew where the cataclysm began—and where it might end.

Brent sensed Danny's presence. A glance at Travis and his partner's nod told him that the miner ghosts remained close, ready to help if called upon. Nonna looked grim and resolute in her black coat and hat. She held the coal sculpture in one hand and an iron knife in the other.

Father Prochazka's bag held an assortment of items he had brought from the church for a doomsday reckoning. He had changed into a black cassock and wore a violet stole, fitting for Last Rites. Obsidian rosary beads looped over his belt, and a silver crucifix hung on a chain around his neck.

Travis still wore the black shirt, jacket, and jeans from the day before. Father Prochazka took a second stole out of his bag and sloshed toward Travis.

"I left the priesthood a long time ago, Padre," Travis protested.

"Thou art a priest forever," Father Prochazka quoted. "I stayed—and quit in all the important ways." He put the stole around Travis's neck. "For luck," he added with a wry half-smile.

The alarm on Brent's watch buzzed. "It's time," he yelled above the wind.

Travis gestured to the dump truck, which backed up as far as it dared toward the sinkhole before tipping its load. Tons of rock salt poured into the abyss, sluiced along by the thousands of gallons of flood waters that swirled and eddied around their feet.

Father Prochazka took a small reliquary from his bag and lifted it to his lips to kiss in blessing before he made the sign of the cross and tossed the holy item into the sinkhole. He began to chant the prayers that made up Last Rites, offering comfort, absolution, and release to the hundreds of souls trapped deep below in tunnels and shafts.

The familiar words of the Act of Contrition carried above the storm as thunder rolled and lightning flashed. He segued into the Apostle's Creed.

Travis began the Rite of Exorcism, baritone to the priest's tenor.

"Exorcizamus te, omnis immundus spiritus, omnis satanica potestas, omnis incursio infernalis adversarii..."

The words seemed to take on new power, joined with the other litany, and Brent felt a shiver that had nothing to do with the rain. He knew their meaning by heart after having faced down demons with Travis. *We exorcise you, every impure spirit, every satanic power, every incursion of the infernal adversary...*

Brent, like the other deputies, stood ready to hold off any interruptions. He gripped his shotgun filled with salt rounds and tried not to vibrate from the combination of cold, fear, and exhaustion. The deputies had their weapons in hand, including iron rebar, just in case all of the tulpas had not been banished, or ghosts from the pit returned for vengeance. They looked as weary and terrified as Brent felt, but they stayed at their posts against an ancient, immortal foe.

Nonna spoke her spells in a strong, sure voice, Italian interweaving with Travis's Latin. Her iron knife cut into the coal figure of the Shubin, paring away layers of the black statue.

A wild howl came from the depths of the pit, unlike anything Brent had heard before. Part wounded creature, part enraged shriek; no one could mistake it for anything human.

Out of the corner of his eye, Brent glimpsed a figure slipping through the crowd, moving ever closer to the edge of the shaft.

Despite the cold, Vinnie wore only a t-shirt and jeans under a clear rain poncho—and a vest packed with explosives.

"Get the hell away from the hole," Calabrese shouted.

"I can't! That thing...the creature—it's in my head," Vinnie yelled back. "My dreams, my thoughts. All the fucking time!"

"Let's talk—" Calabrese attempted.

"No! All it does is scream in my brain. It wants blood. Death. We're linked. And until I end this, it will go on forever." From the depths, the Shubin screeched again.

"We're out of time." Vinnie pushed past, shoving Calabrese out of the way. In two strides, he reached the edge and launched himself over the side.

Father Prochazka shifted to the final portion of the blessing. "Through this holy unction may the Lord pardon thee..."

Travis's voice rose as he neared the end of the exorcism. "...*te rogamus, audi nos!*"

Nonna bellowed a war cry and cut off the head of the coal figure before slamming it to the ground with all her might, bringing her heel down on it hard, watching it splinter and be washed into the sinkhole. *"Essere andato!"*

The ground shook with the force of an explosion deep in the pit.

Lightning arced from the sky, striking deep into the sinkhole, knocking them all off their feet and tossing them away like rag dolls.

Brent struggled to his feet and reached out to give Travis a hand up, wondering if he'd been hit with the psychic shockwave of Vinnie's suicide. Even without Travis's extra abilities, Brent's head throbbed, and his heart pounded.

Don't die on me, Danny's ghost ordered. *Don't you dare die on me. I will throw you back from the afterlife myself.*

The sinkhole widened, forcing everyone to scramble back and away from the yawning pit. Mike Sokolowski abandoned the dump truck, fleeing on foot as the ground beneath the rig crumbled and the vehicle fell into the mine. Flood water poured inside, sweeping leaves and debris along with the torrent. The rain showed no indication of easing, although the thunder and lightning grew more distant.

Brent knelt next to Father Prochazka. The old priest groaned and sat up. "Whaddaya know? I'm not dead," he marveled as Brent helped him to his feet. "Even *I* might be able to get a homily or two out of this," he added with a self-deprecating smile.

"Is the creature gone?" Calabrese asked, finding his voice.

Travis and Nonna frowned in concentration while Brent reached out to his brother. *Danny?*

There are a lot fewer ghosts. The creature has gone so far away I can barely sense him.

"The mine ghosts that remain do so as guardians," Travis said after a moment. "The Shubin is weak and has retreated. I don't think we'll see interference from him for a long time."

Brent nodded in agreement, not quite ready to explain about his ghostly informant.

"The spell I placed on the coal will bind him inside for a long time," Nonna added. "I dare say he may prefer the depths after learning that we can be...unwelcoming."

"You think that explosion is going to make us the next Centralia?" Calabrese asked Mike.

"Dunno. Maybe. But there's a lot of river flowing into that hole and all the other sinkholes—that might save our bacon. We'll monitor. Not gonna worry about it today," Sokolowski said.

Calabrese unholstered a flare gun and shot into the sky. He looked to the others. "Liz and her bunco/bowling group organized a rescue on shortwave radio and walkie-talkies—they've been waiting outside the tunnel until we were sure the spooks weren't going to stop them." He turned to Sokolowski. "We ought to have trucks that can handle the mud ready just in case because that road is going to be a mess."

"I'm on it," Sokolowski said. "And I'll get an update on how we're doing on getting back power and cell coverage."

"Thank you," Calabrese said, looking to everyone who had turned out to help but resting his gaze on Travis, Nonna, Brent, and Father Prochazka. "I have no idea how you did what you did, but it worked. You saved us."

"I think we all worked pretty damn hard to save each other," Travis said. "But right now, I'd wrestle a hellhound for hot coffee and dry clothing."

"We'll get you four where you need to be and take it from here with the cleanup," Calabrese said, indicating for some of the men with trucks to stay and watch the sinkhole while the others headed off to other duties.

The Crown Vic looked no worse for the evening's adventure, still where Travis had parked it. He dropped off Nonna at the library and

Father Prochazka at the rectory so Calabrese could get back to the emergency efforts and promised to check in with them again in the morning.

Brent shivered even with the car's heat turned on high. He didn't know whether that was from nerves or the temperature.

"You're quiet," Travis said after a few minutes.

"Soaked, half-frozen, and newly traumatized. Although for us, same shit, different day."

"Nonna and Father Prochazka came through in a pinch."

"They all did. Feisty little town," Brent replied. "I can see why people like Chris and Liz stay." He paused. "Do you think it's over?"

"From the spooky stuff? Yeah," Travis replied. "Maybe not forever, but for a good long while. Long enough for it to be someone else's problem."

"I think we should take the long way back to Pittsburgh. Maybe stop in Gettysburg, see the battlefield."

"You want to take a medium to one of the most haunted places in the state?"

"Good point. How about Hershey? Chocolate factory, free samples?"

"Works for me. If it's got ghosts, they're probably in a food coma," Travis said.

Brent knew that the banter was proof of life, their way of reassuring themselves and each other that they had made it through another battle. They usually patched up wounds and ordered takeout, so the idea of bingeing on chocolate sounded like a memorable change of pace.

"Looks like everyone's still at Fisher's," Travis said as he found a spot at the edge of the lot. "Let's see how they fared in the apocalypse that wasn't."

CHAPTER ELEVEN

DIM LIGHTING TOLD Travis that Fisher's was still on emergency power. The crowded bar felt subdued, a reminder that its patrons sought refuge instead of entertainment tonight.

"Well? How'd it go?" Chris asked when they made their way inside and found their table reserved and waiting for them.

"It took all of us, but the tulpas are gone, and the Shubin is bound," Brent replied. He was starting to feel both the exhaustion of a high-adrenaline, life-or-death fight and the bruises from having been thrown around by the explosion.

"Did everyone make it back?" Chris gave him a look.

"Everyone except Vinnie. He went full fucking supernatural suicide bomber," Brent answered.

Travis knew his partner was wrestling with guilt over not being able to stop the man's death. "He cut off the Shubin's mental connection, so between his death and the explosion, it probably did help stop the monster," Travis pointed out, trying to give Vinnie his due and ease Brent's self-recrimination.

"Don't blame yourself," Chris said. "Battles have casualties. If this ends South Fork's bad luck streak for a while, it'll be a lot of lives saved." He plunked down a shot of whiskey in front of each of them without waiting for an order and added one for himself. "On the house." He raised his in a toast and clinked glasses with them. "And don't worry about driving—looks like the rain's slacking off finally. We can walk home. You earned it."

Travis felt the alcohol burn down his throat, warming him after the cold, wet night. "How's the crowd handling everything?" The vibe was moody for having just dodged a deadly disaster.

Chris shrugged. "I don't think people believe we're out of the woods yet. River's still rising. The last we heard from Pete, the dam controls still weren't working right. And we haven't accounted for the missing."

"There's a lot of damage. Think people will stay?" Travis looked around at the customers who sat at the bar or huddled at tables. Despite having their town crumble beneath their feet or wash away, they seemed to share a sense of quiet resolve.

"I plan to. I figure that most everyone else will too. After all, it's home."

Chris kept Fisher's open until daybreak. By then, electricity had been restored, the rain had stopped, and the receding flood waters meant those who had taken shelter at the bar could go home to examine the damage.

Despite napping for a few hours in the booth, Travis felt bleary-eyed when they made their way to Chris's house. He peeled off his still-damp clothing and collapsed into bed, not waking until nearly noon to the smell of coffee.

"There are sweet rolls in the oven, plenty of fresh java, and cell signal is back," Brent called from outside his door. "Chris and I have already showered, so the bathroom is all yours."

Travis lingered under the hot water, letting it sluice away the sweat and ash, loosening tight muscles and soothing his battered soul. He dug clean clothes out of his bag, hoped his thick socks would keep him from noticing his still-wet boots, and joined the others in the kitchen.

"Brent recapped the detail of how it went down last night," Chris said. "Thank you. Looks like it was a good call to bring you in."

"Glad we could help," Travis replied.

"So...what now?" Chris sat back and sipped his coffee.

Brent shrugged. "I guess we head back to Pittsburgh once the roads open up, back to our 'other' work."

"This is really what you do?" Chris shook his head. "I mean, to be honest? I feel like you're taking this whole thing too much in stride. Spells, magic, ghosts, shadow creatures...this is all normal for you?"

"Pretty much," Brent replied. "Like Army 'normal.' You train, you go into situations, you get good at navigating hell. Things like what happened here come up, and we hope what we know can help."

Chris was quiet for a moment, giving them both an assessing look. "Well, thank God for that. Because we were screwed, and you made all the difference."

"Sometimes we win. Sometimes..." Brent's voice drifted off, and he looked away.

"Have you heard any news about the dam?" Travis jumped in to shift the topic.

"Pete managed to shunt enough of the dam's overflow to the emergency release pipes. It flowed into the river and made more flooding, but the breastworks held. Soggy basements are better than having the whole damn town wash away," Chris said.

"The mayor put in a request for emergency funding to deal with the sinkholes and mudslides, fix the roads, replace the bridges. It's going to be a while until that's sorted," Chris went on. "Mike and his crew are going to try to clear the debris from at least one of the roads so we can get people out who need help."

"Did Liz's rescue plan work? With the tunnel?" Travis asked.

Chris nodded. "They got here once the sun was up. The Johnstown police sent search and rescue teams through on ATVs. Liz is coordinating with some folks from Johnstown to take care of the people who've lost their homes with the flooding." He smiled fondly. "She's a force of nature."

"You're not going to let her go, are you? She's pretty special." Brent gave his old friend a look.

Chris grinned. "If I got reminded of anything this week, it's that life is short. I'd like to spend the rest of mine with her—if she'll have me."

"You run the best bar in town," Brent joked. "She'd be a fool to pass that up."

"I run the *only* bar in town, but thanks for the vote of confidence."

Travis's phone rang, and he saw Tammy's number. "Are you still in South Fork? Nonna made some coal charms for you. She wanted me to make sure I gave them to you. Can you stop by?"

"Sure," Travis agreed. "She was badass. We couldn't have done it without her."

"She's a humdinger," Tammy agreed.

"How's the crowd at the library?"

"In surprisingly good spirits. The library didn't take any damage —thank Miss Liddie's ghost. We had electric lanterns so when the lights went out, we read bedtime stories and had a sing-along, and then most people found a place to curl up for the night. Today, we're figuring out who can go home and who needs assistance. But that's what a library's for," she said, with a note of pride in her voice.

"I think that being a badass humdinger runs in the family," Travis replied.

Tammy chuckled. "That's high praise."

"How's the sheriff?"

Tammy sighed. "Not bad, considering he hasn't slept in two days. Which means he's grumpy as a bear, snapping at everyone, and calling in favors to get emergency resources. Liz has her whole bunco and bowling gang drafted to find donations for things to get the town back on its feet. It's going to be hard but...I think we might be okay."

From the way Travis had seen the community pull together, he didn't doubt that.

Chris stood and rinsed out his coffee cup. "I should go to the bar, make sure there's no outside damage, and then see how I can help with the clean-up. Take your time—you've earned a break. If you decide to go before I get back, just lock the door behind you, and please stop by the bar if you get hungry later. Oh, and just so you know, you're always welcome here—even if we aren't having an apocalypse."

The house seemed too quiet after Chris left. Travis had noticed Brent's silence but hadn't wanted to ask in front of their host. "Are you okay?"

Brent nodded. "Yeah...I was hoping to hear from Danny. He's been silent since the fight at the sinkhole. He only just came back—I don't want to lose him again."

Travis closed his eyes and focused his gift, looking for Danny's familiar energy. "He's still here," Travis assured Brent. "Just tired. I think he pushed to come back harder and faster than he had the energy to maintain because he wanted to help. Don't feel guilty—that was his choice. But now he needs to rest like we do."

Brent nodded. "Good. I miss him when he's away for too long."

"Speaking of being away, now that the cell phones are back up, I need to let Matt and Jon know what's going on, and you'll need to tell Alex not to panic," Travis said. With the internet, landlines, and cell phones down, he and Brent had been unable to keep their friends updated, and he knew they'd be worried.

"Now we wait for the crews to clear one of the highways out of town," Brent replied with a sigh. "Hope Chris wasn't in a hurry to get rid of us."

Travis and Brent pitched in to help anywhere they could lend a hand. Liz and Tammy were connected to every relief effort in town, helping people get food, shelter, clean water, and other necessities. Once the rain ended, medivac flights took those most in need of care to the nearest trauma centers. Between the storm and the tulpas, there was plenty of work to keep them busy, and keep their minds off everything that had happened.

———

THREE DAYS LATER, road crews broke through, opening one of the roadways.

"Guess we've got to head home," Brent told Chris as he and Travis tossed their bags into the Crown Vic.

"It sure hasn't been boring." Chris grinned. He clasped Brent's forearm and pulled him into a brief hug. "Thanks for answering my Bat-Signal and saving our asses."

"Any time," Brent replied. "But next time, let's make it a social call."

Travis shook hands with Chris. "Call if we can help. I know South Fork's had some bad luck, but there are amazing people here."

Chris nodded. "I know. That's why I stay."

As Travis drove out of town, Brent's phone rang. He frowned at the unfamiliar number and put the call on speaker.

"If you were interested in Dr. Wyrick's research, all you had to do was ask," a man's voice said.

"Who is this?" Brent demanded although Travis feared they both could guess.

"We're impressed by the way you handled the situation," the man continued. "You'd be a strong addition to the team."

"No thanks," Brent growled. "Not now, not ever."

"How long do you think you can stay a free agent? You're going to have to pick a team sooner or later. We can make you a very attractive offer."

Brent looked torn between rage and nausea. "No. Lose my number. I won't change my mind."

"Everything changes," the man replied, with an ominous under-current beneath his too-friendly tone. "And when it does...we'll be here."

The call ended, leaving Brent glaring at his phone.

"Talk to me," Travis said.

"I don't know who that was, or how he got my number—or how

the fuck CHARON knows about us being in South Fork and what we did. I'm furious, and I feel stalked and...shit...I'm scared," Brent confessed.

"And you've got every right," Travis told him. "Bunch of arrogant bastards. But we've already passed along Wyrick's backup notes to Simon, and he'll made sure they got to the Alliance. We stopped what CHARON started here. And you're not alone. I'll do everything I can to keep them away from you—don't forget, we've got some pretty damn powerful friends. We'll keep you safe."

Brent's smile did not reach his eyes. "I know. Thanks. And the call doesn't change a thing. By the time we get back from Hershey, we'll probably have a slew of new cases lined up. Fuck CHARON and the Sinistram. We've got a job to do."

AFTERWORD

It was a lot of fun to be back with Travis and Brent again—and to return vicariously to Western and Central Pennsylvania.

South Fork is a real town. My grandfather was a coal miner there, and my great-grandfather owned a lumber yard there. I haven't been back since I was a teenager, so my description of the town is completely fictitious. Back in the 1930s, Fisher's was a bar there, and people referred to someone who had too much to drink as "leaning toward Fisher's" according to my grandmother.

I love weaving real places and history into the stories. To me, it makes them feel grounded and more believable. I also take authorial liberties to adjust real places to what the story needs. While Fisher's was real once upon a time, it's long gone. Every other business or organization mentioned is not real. I changed details about the geography around South Fork for story purposes, and the tragic, hard luck, supernatural history of the town is completely imaginary.

If "cannelmancy" sounded familiar, we used that type of magic in our Wasteland Marshals book, *Shutdown Crew*.

Travis and Brent will be back with more adventures, so stay tuned!

ACKNOWLEDGMENTS

Thank you so much to my editor, Jean Rabe, to my husband and writing partner Larry N. Martin for all his behind-the-scenes hard work, and to my wonderful cover artist, Lyndsey Lewellen. Thanks also to the Shadow Alliance street team for their support and encouragement and to my fantastic beta readers and the ever-growing legion of beta and ARC readers who help spread the word, including: Andrea, Anne, Barwell, Ben, Candi, Chris, Darrell, Dawn, Debbie, Donald, George, Glen, Grace, Jamie, Janet, Joanne, Kandice, Karen, Karolina, Laurie, Leesil, Miki, and Vikki. And of course, to my "convention gang" of fellow authors for making road trips fun.

ABOUT THE AUTHOR

Gail Z. Martin writes urban fantasy, epic fantasy, and steampunk for Orbit Books, Falstaff Books, SOL Publishing, and Darkwind Press. Urban fantasy series include *Deadly Curiosities* and the *Night Vigil* (Sons of Darkness). Epic fantasy series include *Darkhurst, The Chronicles of The Necromancer, The Fallen Kings Cycle, The Ascendant Kingdoms Saga, and The Assassins of Landria.* Under her urban fantasy MM paranormal romance pen name of Morgan Brice, she has five series (*Witchbane, Badlands, Kings of the Mountain, Fox Hollow,* and *Treasure Trail*) with more books and series to come.

Co-authored with Larry N. Martin are *Iron and Blood,* the first novel in the Jake Desmet Adventures series and the *Storm and Fury* collection; and the *Spells, Salt, & Steel*: New Templars series (Mark Wojcik, monster hunter) as well as *Wasteland Marshals* and *Cauldron: The Joe Mack Adventures.*

Gail's work has appeared in more than forty US/UK anthologies. Newest anthologies include: *The Weird Wild West, Gaslight and Grimm, Baker Street Irregulars, Across the Universe, Release the Virgins, Witches, Warriors,& Wise Women, The Four ???? of the Apocalypse, Nevermore, Three Time Travelers, Christmas at Caynham Castle, Trick or Treat at Caynham Castle,* and *Ring in the New at Caynham Castle.*

Join the Shadow Alliance street team so you never miss a new release! Get the scoop first + giveaways + fun stuff! Also where Gail and Larry get their beta readers and Launch Team! http://www.facebook.com/groups/MartinShadowAlliance

Join the newsletter and get free excerpts at http://eepurl.-
com/dd5XLj Gail is also a con-runner for ConTinual, the online,
ongoing multi-genre convention that never ends. www.Facebook.-
com/Groups/ConTinual

Support Indie Authors

When you support independent authors, you help influence
what kind of books you'll see more of and what types of stories will be
available because the authors themselves decide which books to
write, not a big publishing conglomerate. Independent authors are
local creators, supporting their families with the books they produce.
Thank you for supporting independent authors and small press
fiction!

Deadly Curiosities

Vendetta

Tangled Web

Inheritance

Legacy

Trifles and Folly: Collection

Trifles and Folly 2: Collection

Trifles and Folly 3: Collection

Assassins of Landria

Assassin's Honor

Sellsword's Oath

Fugitive's Vow

Exile's Quest

Outlaw's Vengeance

Night Vigil

Sons of Darkness

C.H.A.R.O.N.

Other books by Gail Z. Martin with Larry N. Martin

Jake Desmet Adventures

Iron & Blood

Spark of Destiny

Storm & Fury: Collection

Spells, Salt, & Steel: New Templars

Spells, Salt, & Steel: Season One

Spells, Salt, & Steel: Season Two

Wasteland Marshals

Wasteland Marshals Volume One

Joe Mack: Shadow Council Archives

Cauldron

Black Sun

Chicagoland

Spellbound